THE PRIVATE WORLDS OF
JULIA REDFERN

BOOKS BY ELEANOR CAMERON

The Mushroom Planet Books
The Wonderful Flight to the Mushroom Planet
Stowaway to the Mushroom Planet
Mr. Bass's Planetoid
A Mystery for Mr. Bass
Time and Mr. Bass

The Julia Books
Julia's Magic
That Julia Redfern
Julia and the Hand of God
A Room Made of Windows
The Private Worlds of Julia Redfern

Other Books for Young People
The Terrible Churnadryne
The Mysterious Christmas Shell
The Beast with the Magical Horn
A Spell Is Cast
The Court of the Stone Children
To the Green Mountains
Beyond Silence

Novel
The Unheard Music

Essays
The Green and Burning Tree: On the Writing
and Enjoyment of Children's Books

ELEANOR CAMERON

THE PRIVATE WORLDS OF JULIA REDFERN

E. P. Dutton New York

Library of Congress Cataloging-in-Publication Data

Cameron, Eleanor, date
  The private worlds of Julia Redfern/by Eleanor Cameron.
—1st ed.
    p.   cm.
Summary: Julia's fifteenth year is filled with jealousy,
forgiveness, first love, and artistic satisfaction, all
against a background of loving support from her adored
uncle, adopted grandmother, and other family members.
  ISBN 0-525-44394-0
  [1. Family life—Fiction.] I. Title.   87-30695
PZ7.C143Pr 1988   CIP
[Fic.]—dc19   AC

Published in the United States by Dutton Children's Books,
a division of Penguin Books USA Inc.
375 Hudson Street, New York, New York 10014

Designer: Barbara Powderly

Printed in the U.S.A.   W   First Edition
10 9 8 7 6 5 4 3 2

for my dear David
and Rita

CHAPTER

1

She was dancing. Music reverberated against the walls. Whirling, unthinking, unseeing, she made her way by memory and instinct between chairs and couch; now looked down, watched her fingers snapping, this side and that, hips swaying, lifted her arms above her head, the music a pulse in her blood: wild music, gypsy music. It possessed her, it *was* her blood; she was drunk on this intoxicating bliss of sound.

"Julia!" She stopped and turned, stared dazedly, as if she'd come out of a trance, at Uncle Phil standing at the door of the living room. "—this abominable racket—no thought for anyone else—I'm *try*ing to work—"

She was astounded at his anger, saw how his eyes blazed and that, absurdly, a wisp of pale brown hair stood up on top of his head as though it too were stiff with indignation. He crossed to the phonograph and snatched the needle from the record. At once she was there.

"You leave our things alone." She heard her voice, low and intense, tremble as his had done. "This is my mother's phonograph, not yours. These are our records—I can play them if I like," and with a darting clutch she wrenched the needle holder from his hand before it could tighten, saw that his hand was shaking, and slammed the needle down. It screeched, with the record still turning, so that she knew she had scratched it, ruined it forever. She shoved it aside and could have struck him with all the hot resentment built up over one small difference, one small crisis after another, during the almost three years since he and Mother had been married when she was twelve.

She turned away. She would not let That One see her cry over her record—a triumph for him—and went to one of the long windows to stare out through a blur down over Berkeley and the bay, struggling for control, knowing she dare not speak.

She heard the click of the record being turned off, his footsteps crossing the room, going to the basement door outside in the hall and down the steps, quick, quick. Couldn't wait to tell Mother working in the back garden— tattletale, like a small boy, she thought with despision: her perfectly good, useful word, not in the dictionary, but what difference? Her word, like "scrapegoat."

"Oh, Julia—" her mother's voice, her mother's eyes, bright with amusement back when Julia was twelve. "Not scrapegoat, dear—scapegoat." Which didn't make sense.

"No, I mean *scrape*goat. Scraped to the bone, bloodied—"

Words had always been her challenge, her fascina-

2

tion, very often her humiliating defeat, and Greg used to chuckle, the superior, knowing older brother with a silly little kid sister.

She turned the record on again, putting the needle beyond the scratch, and music beat across the room as before. That would show him! *That* One, not a real uncle at all but manager of the music store where Mother had worked for years. She danced over and opened the doors onto the sun porch, then those onto the balcony at the back. From there you could look down over the sloping, terraced garden where Mother and Uncle Phil worked every Saturday afternoon after the music store closed, and down across the eucalyptus woods in the ravine that sent up their pungent fragrance in this hot, dry October weather. Here and there in the mass of green, like fingers pointing to the sky, tall chimneys stood, saying that their families still hadn't enough money to rebuild after the fire that destroyed half of Berkeley back when Julia was eleven. She saw in her mind Celia Redfern (but Celia Stanhope now) straightening, lifting her head in amazement.

Abruptly, Julia closed the doors. She no longer felt like dancing. The compulsion was gone and she went back and caught up the needle and turned the record off, then stood for a second or two thinking about Daddy, her own father, killed in the war when she was six. He'd never have shouted; he'd never done that about anything, but suffered his griefs and disappointments and angers almost in silence. About the phonograph, "Turn it down, will you, Julia? It's too loud," knowing that of course she would. How much she had loved him! They'd understood one another.

"You *will* be a writer—like me," he'd said just before he went off to France to be an airplane pilot. "No, not like me," he'd corrected himself sharply. "Lord, no," because of the big tan envelopes with his writings in them always coming back from the magazines he'd sent them to. If he were here now, they would have talked about her own writing.

She turned and went to the top of the basement stairs and shouted, "Greg!" Silence. He was gone from his room down there. Frustrated, she went to the front door, banged it behind her, and ran off down the hill, having a furious need to talk to her friend Rhiannon Moore, who'd been all over the world, met everybody, done everything, had had a famous poet as a lover and now a son a famous pianist. She ran all the way down the slope to Shattuck Avenue, then walked very fast along one street and then another to Rhiannon's place.

The big old barn-red house was still buried in a wild mass of greenery even though Oren, Rhiannon's son, had sent her a check to have a gardener come and cut the grass back and front and prune the bushes and trees. A disgrace, it all looked, said Rhiannon's sister to Julia and Celia one day. But then Rhiannon, she said, never seemed to care about appearances. It was so embarrassing. Rhiannon would have lifted an eyebrow and shrugged.

Julia ran up the steps and stood at the front door listening before she rang. But that wasn't Rhiannon playing. Maybe Oren, one of his records? Not a record belonging to him, but Oren *on* a record. Prickles—no, chills—went up and down her arms. It was what this kind of playing did to her, though there was always the other excitement simmering up when she stood on Rhiannon's porch waiting for the door to open. The confidences! Julia would make toast and coffee and bring up the tray to the music room, where they would talk about everything, about Julia's writing, and about life and love: the relationships between men and women. She sometimes felt there was nothing she couldn't tell Rhiannon, no question she couldn't ask.

She rang, and in a moment the door swung open and there was Rhiannon Moore. But not in a housecoat as she often was at this time of the afternoon, having worked all day at the piano except for a half hour or so to settle on the couch with something to eat. She had on a bronze-colored skirt and a pale green shirt. Her hair, dark streaked with gray, was combed back and up and done in a high fold. And she had on big lustrous earrings and a medallion on a silvery-gold chain swinging against her shirt. Mr. Yeats, her poet, had given her the medallion like a piece of frozen seawater years ago in Ireland when Rhiannon had been in love with him. (And he with her, as she with him? But that had never been gone into. It was always, "When I was in love with Mr. Yeats." Or sometimes she called him Willie.)

Julia stared. She had never seen Rhiannon so handsome, except perhaps that night she'd taken Julia, almost three years ago, over to the Tivoli, across the bay, to hear Oren play with the San Francisco Symphony.

"Julia! Why, it's magic. I was going to call you, and here you are. Come in, come in—" and her arms went around Julia, and she hugged her with a child's impulsive delight while the music rolled down the stairs.

"It isn't—that isn't a record!"

"No." Rhiannon stood there, her eyes shining as if she were harboring a secret. "It *isn't* a record."

"Not—you don't mean—"

"Yes! He's been here with me for three days, resting and practicing, all private—nobody knows, not a soul— before he goes home to Ireland the day after tomorrow. And, Julia, I'm going with him."

"Not to stay!"

"Oh, don't look so bereft—of course not. I couldn't stay in that big Irish barracks of his all by myself while he's away on tour, as he is most of the time. Just for a month or so, it'll be, while he gets himself ready for the next string of concerts. Isn't it exciting! Now, come on up. Will you take the tray for me? It's just to make him stop for a little and talk. We've been having something in the middle of the afternoon, and then we don't have anything else until late."

But Julia backed against the door. "No, I couldn't. Not looking like this, my old dress, my hair not combed." To be looked at by Oren Moore specifically, she meant, for whom people bought tickets weeks in advance and elegantly dressed women crowded backstage after the concert to exclaim about him and flatter him in their high,

6

silly voices. Julia mimicked them to Uncle Hugh and Aunt Alex after the Tivoli, and Uncle Hugh had been highly amused, but large, beautiful Aunt Alex looked straight at Julia without so much as a smile, Uncle Hugh having abysmally forgotten to get tickets for the two of them. No doubt of it, she'd have reveled in being one of those women. "Oh, Oren, my dear—" laying her hand lightly on his arm. A close, privileged friend. "It was marvelous, simply marvelous!" And then they'd all have gone to Aunt Alex's house (a very impressive one, high up above San Francisco) for a little intimate celebration, just a few very special people, Aunt Alex had planned, because of the friendship, so extraordinary and even almost unbelievable, between Mrs. Moore, *Oren Moore's mother*, and Julia! But it hadn't turned out like that, and Aunt Alex had been extremely cool to Uncle Hugh for at least three days after the performance as a punishment for his idiocy.

"What do you mean?" demanded Rhiannon. "Looking like what? You look just as you should—windblown, naturally. Nothing wrong with that, and I'll be very disappointed if you refuse. I've talked about you, what fun we have together and the good discussions."

So Julia took the tray and followed Rhiannon upstairs, her heart thudding, remembering how Oren Moore had looked at her when Rhiannon took her backstage to introduce her.

They came into the music room and Julia put the tray down on the coffee table. She stood waiting at one of the low, round-topped windows with their pale amber panes that sent an unearthly glow almost like moonlight across the room from the white roof of the de Rizzios' house next door, where she and Celia and Greg used to live before Uncle Phil came along.

Oren was thundering at the piano, his lean body, whose every cell must have been concentrated into the force pouring onto the keyboard, curved over it. Now there came a quiet place, a rippling of pure, clear, tender notes that went on until passion and force heaved up again like a wave into the final chords. He sat for a moment, motionless, went back over the ripple of notes, over them again, then stopped suddenly at the chink of cup and saucer, stood up and turned—and there he was, just as she remembered him.

CHAPTER

2

He had dark, almost black eyes, deep set in a thin face. He was very like his mother. And those dark, concentrating eyes did her the courtesy of looking at her, not politely or indifferently or out of duty to please Rhiannon, but seriously took her in as an individual human being worthy of attention, just as he had in that crush of people at the Tivoli.

"So it's Julia again," and he came over and held out his hands and took hers in both of his while she lost her breath. "But you're so much taller! You're different! Do you know what that was I was playing?"

"Oh, yes," and she just managed a steady voice. "Mrs. Moore's played it for me. It's one of her favorites." But her cheeks burned to be informing Oren Moore about his own mother.

"So it is," said Rhiannon, "and so I have, in a way, you

ght say. Played it, I mean. But you've really heard it only now. Strange, I used to think, some time ago, to have your own child outdistance you by light-years at your own work."

"Do you forgive me, Mother? Being a public person?"

She laughed and sat down on the couch behind the fat earthenware teapot. "What I do here, day after day, is struggle along behind you, thinking of you with nothing but joy. Now come, my two favorite people, and sit down and be comfortable."

There were thin chicken sandwiches and fruitcake with thick lemon butter icing. And Julia remembered the time she had gone up to Dr. and Mrs. Penhallow's to hear Mrs. Penhallow, the editor of the children's page of the *Gazette*, tell her what a fine story "The Mask" was, and there had been also all those wonderful things to eat in the middle of the afternoon so that by night she could scarcely look at her dinner.

All at once, in the midst of their laughter and chatter about one thing and another, Rhiannon turned. "Julia, I've just this minute thought, we won't be here to see you at the Greek Theatre."

"The Greek Theatre! Doing what?" demanded Oren.

"Well, acting," said Julia, "I suppose you could say. But not in a whole play." Imagine even mentioning what she was to do in front of Oren Moore.

"But of course you'll be acting," said Rhiannon.

"Yes, well, I suppose I will. But mine's just one of a lot of scenes. It's a dramatic festival. All the high schools in the bay area are sending one boy and one girl to do scenes from Shakespeare's plays. I'm to be Lady Macbeth for ours, and one of the fellows, John Naismith, is to be Hamlet."

"Lady Macbeth—but that's not an easy role," said Oren. "What lines will you do?"

"Say them for us," exclaimed Rhiannon. "Why not? I'm so disappointed I won't be here after all. Couldn't you do them for us now?"

But not in front of this man, who must have seen all of Shakespeare's plays acted by the greatest actors. She shook her head. She would make a fool of herself.

"But, Julia," pressed Rhiannon, "you're going to have to say your lines in front of thousands of people—"

"Not thousands!" protested Julia. Rhiannon, with her rich, rather husky voice and expressive face, was a great one for dramatic exaggeration. "Maybe hundreds," she said.

The Moores had to smile at Julia's precision. "Well, hundreds, then, but what difference." Rhiannon waved a hand. "Here you have two people, sympathetic friends— you don't have a thing to worry about. And besides," she finished, as if this entirely settled the matter, "It'll be one more good chance to rehearse before next Sunday."

"Quite," said Oren with finality. "Up you get, Julia."

So Julia, her heart thudding faster than when she had climbed the stairs with the tea tray, got up and went over to stand with her back to the grand piano, waiting for her breathing to settle. Oren and Rhiannon seemed to understand, because they, too, waited quietly.

"You are eaten by ambition," she could hear little Mr. Winter saying at school. His fiery blue eyes were fixed on her, piercing her, his small, lined face tense with determination to make her feel and understand to the core the

11

meaning of her part. His sparse gray hair was all rumpled with being tugged, heaped up, scraped across his head as he explained and took the various parts with incredible energy, and pushed them—Julia and then John Naismith—around the stage. "You are cold," he said to her of Lady Macbeth. "Not physically, though perhaps that, too, but with a deadly inner coldness. You must be adamant as ice, completely pitiless."

"There are two groups of lines," said Julia to Rhiannon and Oren. "In the first, Lady Macbeth is calling on the spirits to do as she commands. Then the chorus tells briefly, in a kind of menacing chant, what goes on between the time of her calling on the spirits and her sleepwalking scene."

She drew a breath, looking off into the distance, hands clenched at her waist, and began.

> Come you spirits
> That tend on mortal thoughts—

No," she broke off, "not right. Too high. I have to get lower." She began again, bringing her voice up strongly "from that dark cavern," Mr. Winter called it, "of Lady Macbeth's remorseless hardness and power."

> Come you spirits
> That tend on mortal thoughts, unsex me here,
> And fill me, from the crown to the toe, top-full
> Of direst cruelty. . . .
>
> . . . Come to my woman's breasts,
> And take my milk for gall, you murdering ministers,
> Wherever in your sightless substances

You wait on nature's mischief! Come, thick night,
And pall thee in the dunnest smoke of hell,
That my keen knife see not the wound it makes,
Nor heaven peep through the blanket of the dark
To cry "Hold, hold!"

She stood silent for a moment, then turned and went
off to the side, turned again and came slowly back, wring-
ing her hands, rubbing them together in fierce desperation "as if you would rub the skin from them with a look
of utmost revulsion on your face," she heard Mr. Winter
saying. "You're jangled in the mind by now, Julia. You've
committed the murder, the spirits have used you as
you commanded them, and you're exhausted after hounding and hounding Macbeth without letup. All vitality
and reason have drained away. You're sick in your soul
with the sight and smell of blood and slaughter, with all
you've been driven to do—all you've driven yourself
to do. Remember this when you groan out your 'Oh's,'
Julia. They're wrung out of that bone-deep sickness."

Yet here's a spot. . . . Out, damned spot! out, I say! One;
two. Why then 'tis time to do't. Hell is murky. Fie, my lord,
fie! a soldier, and afeard? What need we fear who knows it,
when none can call our power to account? Yet who would
have thought the old man to have had so much blood in him?
. . . The Thane of Fife had a wife. Where is she now? What,
will these hands ne'er be clean? No more o' that, my lord,
no more o' that! You mar all with this starting. . . . Here's the
smell of the blood still: All the perfumes of Arabia will not
sweeten this little hand. Oh, oh, oh! . . . Wash your hands,
put on your nightgown, look not so pale! I tell you yet again,

Banquo's buried. He cannot come out on's grave. . . . To bed, to bed! There's a knocking at the gate. Come, come, come, come, give me your hand! What's done cannot be undone. To bed, to bed, to bed!

There was a silence. Julia walked away, then stood looking at Rhiannon and Oren.

"Why, Julia!" cried Rhiannon in amazement, "I never *thought*—!" and she and Oren clapped and clapped, and Julia felt blissful relief, knowing she had done as well as she possibly could. She had astonished herself, remembering precisely all Mr. Winter's directions for each movement during that last long speech.

"Splendid!" exclaimed Oren. "I mean it—for a young one. You were splendid. Who's been directing you?"

"Our high school drama teacher, Mr. Winter. He's a marvelous little man, no taller than I am. He loves Shakespeare as if he'd actually known him, like someone on the highest pedestal of all who deserves every ounce of work we can give him. Mr. Winter never lets us get away with the least sloppiness or slackness."

"It shows," said Oren. "I like very much how quietly and strongly you speak during the first speech, how you never move from one spot, keeping your hands clenched together except when you say, 'Come to my woman's breasts.' You project all that merciless determination from a kind of pillar of burning stillness, which I think is much more effective and ominous than throwing yourself around. Congratulations to your Mr. Winter."

Julia grinned at him. "It reminds me of your playing—

the way you don't swoop at the keys, then sway backwards with your head lifted and your eyes closed, then swoop again and work yourself around on the piano bench. I like it that you don't do that."

Oren and Rhiannon shouted with laughter, "because Oren has a friend who does exactly that," Rhiannon said, "but he's a superb pianist."

"Now," said Oren, "you've put on a performance for us, Julia, and I'd like to do something for you. What shall it be—let me think."

"I know," she said. She remembered waking in what seemed the depths of the night when there would be the ghostly sound of Rhiannon playing, the notes falling like drops of water, she'd thought then, and so often in a minor key. What a curious, unexplainable bliss the sound of Rhiannon playing very softly like that in the midnight silence would bring her as she lay there looking up through the skylight of her room upstairs, next door, at the stars scattered across her patch of the night sky. Heavenly to lie there listening to Rhiannon and then drifting off to sleep. "Your mother's pieces—the two she was composing when I lived at the de Rizzios'—I used to hear her playing them, very slow and haunting."

"Yes—slow and haunting. I was going over them this morning."

Julia settled beside Rhiannon, and Oren went to the piano, sat down, and commenced. But Rhiannon had never played her own compositions like this. Julia turned to glance at her and she had an expression on her face not to be described: *her work*, brought to perfection by her own flesh and blood. When he had finished one, he waited a moment, then went on to the other. And from the way he played, you could feel his respect, just as if this were the work of some great composer. And when he'd finished, he turned on the bench and looked at Rhiannon.

"I never told you this morning how much I admire what you've done—"

Rhiannon had to wait a moment before she could speak. "Well," she said shakily, "now I'm out of my misery. I've been wanting to know."

The clock on the mantel chimed and Julia stood up. "Six! And it'll be half past by the time I get home." She went over to Oren. "Thank you very much, Mr. Moore."

He put his hands on her shoulders and leaned down and kissed her on the cheek. Startled, she saw him glance over her head, and his eyes must have met his mother's, whereupon he let out a little indulgent, teasing laugh and ruffled Julia's hair as if she were around five.

Instantly, without the slightest warning to herself, she was filled with fury. She gave him a look, said goodbye in a stifled voice, and turned and left.

CHAPTER

3

Julia went to the basement stairs, leapt down two at a time to Greg's room and stood at the open door. There he was, crouched lankily over his typewriter, Daddy's old one that Uncle Hugh had had overhauled for him, rattling along in a mad torrent the way he always typed. Another of his fat letters to Leslie, it would be, because she was in France for a year with her mother and father, who was on sabbatical leave from the university. Sabbatical leave: something, said Leslie, whose father taught there, that professors get every seven years.

They wrote pages and pages back and forth, she and Greg, as if some sort of hunger were being appeased, Mother said to Uncle Phil one night when Greg was out. "What can they be about—all those pages! But of course we'll never know, the way Greg keeps their letters strictly to himself." He'd been morosely quiet after Leslie left, and that was when the first long one was written.

"Maybe they're meant for each other," Julia had said, meaning Leslie with her poetry and Greg with his Egyptians. Often they'd closet themselves down here in Greg's room, where his large Egyptian drawings, done in pen and ink and watercolor on the very finest and thickest Strathmore paper, were pinned to the walls. And one of Celia and Uncle Phil's birthday gifts, the head and shoulders of Queen Nefertiti, stood on the top of his bookcase over the desk, from where she gazed serenely out of tilted, almond-shaped eyes at some ancient scene with a half smile that spoke of pleasures secret to herself. You could hear them, Leslie and Greg, laughing over their own odd little jokes. Strangely, Julia couldn't be jealous, considering the fact that Leslie had started out her own friend; somehow Leslie managed that she needn't be.

"Meant for each other! At their ages?" Celia had to laugh. "Why, they're nothing but children, Julia, with their whole lives ahead of them."

"They're sixteen. And if they're children, what am I?" At fourteen, almost fifteen, Julia didn't at all think of herself as a child. Celia, tactfully, made no reply.

"Greg," said Julia.

The torrent stopped and he turned and studied her disapprovingly, pushed his glasses up his beaky nose with that quick, habitual gesture of his, then pulled them way down and peered at her over them as if he were an old man: his private brand of humor. He'd always used to be Professor Cranley. "Obviously, I'm occupied."

"Oh, occupewed a pie," said Julia, not to be put off. "You told me a lie."

"I've never told you a lie. There'd be no point. If I didn't want to tell you something, I wouldn't."

Well, that was true. All the same, "You lied, when we were on the ferry going to San Francisco that time Mother sent me over with you so that she could think about getting married. You said Daddy never had a single thing published in his whole life, and he did. You were old enough to remember. You must have been eight—"

"Yes," he said, "I do remember."

"So why did you lie?"

His eyes behind his glasses were extraordinarily large, deep brown, almond-shaped like Nefertiti's and her husband, the Pharaoh Ikhnaton's. Those eyes came up and met hers for a moment. Then he folded his arms on the edge of his desk. It was Daddy's, and Greg had had it all these years and no doubt would always have it, with its tall bookcase back filled with his books on Egypt: a passion since before he was twelve. "I didn't have any idea of lying. The fact is, I guess, I meant nothing big, probably. No book."

Julia studied him in cold indignation. "What about short-story writers? You mean they've never published anything because all they write is stories?"

Greg adjusted his glasses upward and seemed to consider. "I haven't got an explanation. I remember now Mom sending a story of his off after he was shot down, and it was taken."

"Yes, and it was just as if," pursued Julia mercilessly, "you and Mother had hatched up a little plot to change me about him, to make him less than Uncle Phil, because as it happens I remember now some things *she* said. But it didn't work."

"We didn't have any plot, Jule."

"He got furious at me this afternoon—That One," said Julia, "for playing a record and dancing."

Greg sighed. "Not for playing the record and dancing, I'll bet, but because of the racket when he was no doubt tussling with the music store's overdue accounts out in the breakfast room. I heard it, the racket, and you galumphing around—"

"I *never* galumph," said Julia, stung.

"—galumphing around and turning the record on and off. I thought you'd gone mental. And then he came charging down and went out back—"

"Where he's been at it, I'll bet anything, about what a stubborn, disobedient, self-willed chit I am. And I won't be made to apologize for nothing. He made me scratch my record, and I *hate* him!" The passion in her voice startled even Julia.

"So," said Greg, "you're back where you started before they got married, and you're still a selfish kid. Why don't you try giving in now and then and making it easier for everybody? Why can't you let Mom be happy? She could be if it weren't for you." Greg said this quietly and evenly. He, like Daddy, had never been in the habit of lashing out.

Julia stared at him. She felt as if she'd been hit in the pit of the stomach, remembering some time, somewhere, when Mother had said, "I can't be happy, really happy about my marriage unless I have your blessing." "Well, then," Julia had answered, "you have it," because she loved Celia and wanted her to be happy.

But her mother had never had it, that blessing, not really, perhaps not even for a moment. And so it wasn't Greg who had lied, at least not knowingly and purposefully, but Julia herself. She went back upstairs and into the front hall and there was Celia rounding the corner from her bedroom.

"Oh, Julia—*there* you are—" and her face lighted.

"Yes, here I am."

Celia had a smudge of dirt across her cheek, streaks of what appeared to be grayish chalk across the front of her old skirt, and strands had come loose from the long fold that caught back her thick brown hair. Julia's, from its auburn red when she was small, was turning dark like Celia's. Why, she's happy, it struck Julia, so what had Greg been going on about?

"We've finished the lower wall along the terrace at the bottom, Uncle Phil and I. Look at me, cement on my skirt and my hair all coming down—Julia, what is it? You look— I don't know—suppressed, somehow, and stewing. What is it?"

"Nothing." She went into her bedroom and Celia followed.

"Come, now, there *is* something!" She sat on the bed and studied Julia, who was flung back on it, face up, hands folded on her stomach. Julia thought for a moment before answering.

"I've been down at Mrs. Moore's. I did my Lady Macbeth for her." She had no intention of telling about that

21

hypocrite Oren Moore and all the fun they'd had, and how he'd treated her as if she were actually worthy of attention and respect, just as if she were an adult, and then finished off with that odious, teasing laugh and the hair ruffling. "Mother, why did you and Greg try to put me off about Daddy before you married Uncle Phil, trying to make him seem so much less than Uncle Phil, as if the two of you had some sort of little plot worked out?"

Celia stared at her. "Was that what you and Rhiannon Moore talked about, Greg and me and how we cooked up a little plot to put down Daddy to you because of Uncle Phil? I'm astonished at you."

Julia kept her eyes on the ceiling. "I never mentioned any such thing to Mrs. Moore, and wouldn't. I don't talk about you behind your back. Well, maybe I do once in a while, but only to Greg. I found Daddy's story last night, that was published in *The Listener*. Remember?"

"Of course."

"Well, the instant I saw it, I remembered Greg saying once that Daddy never had a single thing published in his whole life. And that was a lie. And you said that I kept Daddy's picture on my desk only from the minute you decided to marry Uncle Phil. And you said that Daddy was difficult to love sometimes—and I couldn't believe it. He wasn't *ever* hard for me to love, even when he went all dark and disappeared down onto the wharves for his long walks when he was having a hard time and not getting things published. Being a writer myself, I guess I understand him where you might not have."

Celia was quiet, gazing at Julia as if not seeing her,

22

apparently going back in her mind and recalling things quite differently from the way Julia was telling it. "I never hatched up a plot with Greg to spoil your memory of Daddy. I couldn't have."

"Then why did you say those things to me? Didn't you love Daddy?"

"*Julia!*"

"I thought you did. It took you an awfully long time to get over his death. That's what Gramma always said."

Celia looked away. "Yes, it did. And just remember that I *did* love Daddy. I loved him very much. And now I love Uncle Phil, but differently." Julia made no reply. "You see, I wanted a mate, and companionship. I needed one. I didn't want to go on alone." Still Julia could find nothing to say. Her own mother *needed* a mate. What did she mean exactly? That she needed—? But to imagine her and Uncle Phil— No! At once, Julia shut the door on her mother's privacy. "Will you come out and help me get dinner?"

"I don't want any. Mrs. Moore had tea and things to eat, but I'll come in a minute and help."

That night Julia took a key from the drawer of the small wicker desk she'd inherited from Celia. At the de Rizzios', next door to Rhiannon's house, it had stood in Celia's bedroom when Julia had her own desk under the two big windows from which she looked across the drive to Rhiannon's music room. That low desk, that her father had made for her when she was six, now stood next to her bed and held her lamp, at the end nearest her pillow, and whatever books she might have from the library, as well as the framed photograph of her father she had spoken of to Celia.

She unlocked the desk's shallow middle drawer and took from it her *Book of Strangenesses,* the fat leather-bound journal Uncle Hugh had given her on her eleventh birthday and that she had at first found so hard to write in because it was too grand. "Intimidating," a word back then to add to her collection of especially valuable ones like "inconsolable" and "subtle" and "apprehensive" and "insinuating." Intimidating. Yes. Because just the sight of her wretched writing, as it began defiling the first creamy page, was almost unbearable. But as time went on she took courage, became accustomed, or perhaps hardened, and went charging ahead, page after page, and now the book was almost filled with her scrawls and she would soon need another.

October 15

When I was out in the hall at Rhiannon's this afternoon, after I'd flamed up at Oren and hardly said goodbye to him, she followed me while Oren sat right down and began practicing again as if he'd never been interrupted. Or as if he was thankful *that* was over. We—she and I—stood at the head of the stairs for a second or two and I felt she was embarrassed. She followed me down neither of us saying a word and I had the strongest feeling that Rhiannon was thinking all sorts of things about Oren's kiss and my stiffness. He was leading a mere child to think he might have some special feeling for me and she disapproved. And he'd caught her eye and tried to cover everything by laughing and treating me like a little kid.

But when we got to the bottom she put her arms around me. "I won't see you again, Julia, before I go." And then suddenly we were easy with each other and there was no undercurrent. When I stood back she gave me a fond, studying look. "We've been friends for a long time," she said, "and I've come to the end of being Mrs. Moore. I want to be Rhiannon to you. Will you call me that?" And she asked me about my writing. So far, *St. Nicholas*, she remembered, has published "The Mask" and "The Last of the Bayaderes," about the East Indian dancers, and "The Young Princess," about Elizabeth Tudor's death as a child in the Great Plague and her secret replacement by her playmate Edward Neville. Which explains why Queen Elizabeth never married and why she had such a high, naked forehead. She was going bald the way men do—she *was* a man! "So now what, Julia? What's next?"

I'm over it, my fury at Oren. But I'll be glad when I'm fifteen. On the Saturday after this, a week from today, the day before the Greek Theatre, I'll be meeting Uncle Hugh for lunch at the Green Door in San Francisco and this will be the first time we've ever had my birthday lunch alone. But you know, I think I'll go early and catch Uncle Hugh at the art school so I can watch him in class, drawing from the nude.

CHAPTER

4

Over in San Francisco, at the top of the hill, Julia crossed the paved courtyard of the art school, shaded by a huge old peppertree, went around to the front entrance, and entered the broad main hall. Sunlight slanted through enormous, bare, dusty windows across bare floors and onto drawings and watercolors pinned to the pine walls. There was a special smell in this old building: linseed oil, turpentine, dust, still lifes of once fresh flowers and fruit past their prime, fixative, and the fragrance of pine walls and floorboards soaking in the heat of the sun.

She heard a woman's laugh, low and excited, and she recognized that the man standing at the far end of the hall with a woman was Uncle Hugh. Julia stopped at one of the windows not far from them in order to determine who this woman might be. She was slender and had short, curly dark hair cut like a boy's with her ears showing. She turned her face toward Julia for a second, then looked back up at Uncle Hugh. And Julia knew in that momentary glimpse that she was neither pretty nor beautiful yet somehow queerly attractive in spite of the fact that her profile showed a slightly too large nose.

She was apparently telling something wryly amusing, because every now and then she let out a rather mocking laugh and Uncle Hugh would smile but did not ever laugh in return. He seemed to be watching the teller with even more attention then he was giving her story—perhaps enjoying the way she was telling it. She moved her hands, darted them about, shaping her story, then suddenly clasped them at some climactic moment and put her head back and shut her eyes as if it was all too much. She was dramatist and actress in one.

Now Julia lifted her arm and rested her elbow on the windowsill, and Uncle Hugh must have caught the sudden movement out of the corner of his eye. He turned and stared at her in astonishment, and the young woman, too, stopped and turned, perhaps not at all pleased, Julia felt, that she had been cut off and attention diverted.

"Hello, Uncle Hugh." Julia went to him and slid her arm through his. "I didn't want to interrupt—I was waiting."

"But, Julia, I thought we were to meet at the restaurant. What a surprise." Not a nice surprise? Was he irked?

"I wanted to watch you painting or drawing—whatever class I could walk in on—"

"But you're too late for that, and you couldn't have watched in the last class. We're drawing from the nude, and they don't allow anyone not a student to come in. Julia, this is Mrs. Haydn, just back from her travels. Nikki, this is my niece, Julia Redfern. We always have her birthday luncheon together," he explained to this now watchful person who was absorbing Julia with interest, a woman with pale, clear skin, large eyes of such a dark blue as to be almost navy, and a wide mouth with full, expressive lips.

"I'm sorry," Julia said, "if I interrupted your story." But at least Uncle Hugh wasn't annoyed. He'd put his hand over hers, resting on his arm. "I was going to stay quiet until you'd finished."

Nikki didn't reply at once. But now one lively eyebrow flicked up and she shrugged and smiled oddly by pursing her lips a little. "Doesn't matter, Julia—doesn't matter in the least. I think I'd finished. So long, Hugh. Be seeing you," and she turned from them and walked off along the hall the way Julia had come.

Uncle Hugh, looking after her, called out, "So long, Nikki—until next week." And with her back to them, walking away, never turning her head, she lifted a hand and waved it.

"Who is she, Uncle Hugh?" for now Nikki had turned the corner and was gone. Yet even as she asked, Julia had the strangest sense of something familiar, though even more strange was the fact that she was seeing herself and Mama (Mama then, not Mother—how many years ago?) sitting on the deck of a ferry, talking. But why Mama,

28

why the ferry? What had that scene to do with Nikki? It was all vague, momentary, fleeting.

"Who is Nikki Haydn?" said Uncle Hugh. "Come, let me show you a painting."

He took her to the door of the art school office, and there, over the secretary's desk at the back, was a large painting of Nikki: a three-quarter view, as if she'd been caught in the act of turning suddenly toward the painter, her right hand out in an impulsive gesture, and the whole thing swimming in light, a warm light that turned her skin golden. She had on a magenta sweater or shirt (the brush strokes were loose, so that it wasn't possible to tell which), and the glimpse of skirt was a rich blackish-green. She was half smiling, but there was something about that smile, a hint of something secret, and in the expression of the eyes, something evasive that was puzzling in relation to the outheld hand. Yes, but the hand was held palm down, not up.

"I don't like it," said Uncle Hugh abruptly. "It's Nikki, but it's a side I don't see. Where's her humor and her wit? Her merriment and delight in things? Not there—not a glimmer. She's the daughter of the man who owns the school, who started it. Her husband, Ted Haydn, painted the picture years ago. He teaches here—I've had classes with him."

"You don't like him."

Uncle Hugh reflected for a moment. "You're a quick one, Julia. And you're quite right. He's difficult, let's say. Demanding. Impatient. Tempery. And it's hard to take because he has such force and assurance. But he's gifted—God knows the man's gifted. Well, as you can see. I always felt wrung out when he was through with me, with his criticism of my work. Come on, let's be off. I want to know if you're ready for tomorrow."

They sat at one of the window tables in the flowery, fern-hung room with its big wicker chairs, "their" table that Uncle Hugh always arranged for, where they could look out from this ninth floor restaurant over the city and the blue water of the bay to the far side, to Oakland and Berkeley at the foot of their low hills. She'd been telling him about saying her lines to the Moores, and how they'd applauded, and Oren Moore had played— especially for her, in return for her performance—Rhiannon's two pieces.

Uncle Hugh's face lighted with astonishment, then amusement suffused with just a hint of malice. "Marvelous! Wait till your Aunt Alex hears—wait'll you see her expression. Oren Moore!" He chuckled with delight. "She won't be able to bear it, but I won't say a word. You must tell her yourself, tell us all, when we come to your place tomorrow after the Greek Theatre." He reached down beside his chair and brought up the wrapped box he'd gotten from the trunk of his car and carried under his arm as he came in. "Happy Birthday, Julia," and he kissed the tip of his fingers and laid them lightly against her cheek—quickly, a little impulsive gesture, but she caught his hand and held it for a moment.

He is my father, she thought, as she let it go. Ever since my father was killed he's been my father and I love him as if he were. We're of a kind. She took the box and her hands dropped, holding it, because it was so much heavier than she'd thought it would be. Not a nightgown, then, or a pair of pajamas or a sweater. No—she knew by the weight what it was.

Just as last time, they gave their orders to the waitress before Julia tore off the ribbon and paper and lifted the lid, and there, as she knew it would be, was another leather-bound volume with *The Private Journal of Julia Redfern* pressed in gold on the cover, but on the title page was lettered *The Book of Strangenesses, Volume II.*

"Greg told me," said Uncle Hugh, "that that's what you call it. Not a journal. Why *The Book of Strangenesses*? I like it—but why?"

"Haven't I ever explained? But I suppose I never thought to. It's because I'm always being surprised by strangenesses, by what happens to me, as if I'm always turning a corner and never can imagine exactly what lies ahead. So strange, Uncle Hugh—everything. I've always felt I'll never get used to it, that I should be alive and the world the way it is, the things that happen we never could guess. I've wondered if other people feel this way, but I'd never ask. It's too personal, like asking suddenly if they believe in God. Do you understand?" And then the next words came unbidden to Julia's tongue. "I liked meeting Nikki. I remember her name."

His eyes came up, startled. "Do you, now? How could you possibly? And why should you have liked meeting her?"

"Because you took me up someplace when I was little—someplace you used to stay before you were married—and you showed me the exact spot where Aunt Alex proposed to you. D'you remember, Uncle Hugh, taking me to your apartment or room or whatever it was? It had a fireplace and big windows with a view. And you told me about Nikki." Julia waited for him to answer; what could he be thinking? Now the waitress put down their salads and the basket of enormous hot popovers (of which Julia planned to have three, plus dessert) wrapped in a napkin.

"Good lord, Julia, you must have been a mere infant, not more than six or seven."

"Maybe, but some time. I remember you said, or how would I know, because Mother never told me, being so strict about private affairs, that you were going to marry Nikki and then Aunt Alex had her own way and got you instead. And I badgered Mother about it—yes, now I remember—and wanted her to explain about a woman asking the man instead of the other way around, and she said they don't do it. But Aunt Alex did." Julia leaned toward him and gave a little teasing laugh at Uncle Hugh's expression. "She was determined to get you. And you had to tell Nikki out in the garden one night, and she said, 'Alex always gets her own way, doesn't she?' and went into the house and you never saw her again. Not until now, is that it? Oh, I thought about it as a child, making up the whole thing, how it must have been: seeing you walking up and down in the dark in the garden, or perhaps in the moonlight—I think I made it moonlight—before going up to the door, having to tell

Nikki." Did you love them both, Uncle Hugh—was that it? came to her tongue to ask, but something stopped her.

Uncle Hugh gazed at her, appalled. "My God, Julia, what a ferocious, consuming, merciless memory you have. A person isn't safe around you—though, as a matter of fact, it didn't happen exactly like that."

"But tell me—Nikki isn't mad at you anymore, not after all this time, I can see that. She's forgiven you and married Ted Haydn instead. You say he's difficult—"

"Yes. They've been divorced and now they're trying to get back together again. He's been here, teaching on and off, but Nikki's been—oh, all over the place, France, Italy, roundabout. What she was telling me," he said, and then was silent for a little as if going over what had happened, "was about their latest set-to. And these'll go on, these blowups, considering their natures. The two of them!" He shook his head.

Julia was suddenly overcome with shyness. Obviously, she couldn't tell Uncle Hugh everything, ask him any question, as she'd always thought. Because what she wanted to ask, but couldn't, was: Why had he given in and let Nikki go? This she would never understand. Ever since she'd stopped taking his and Aunt Alex's marriage for granted, she'd wondered why he had ever married her in the first place, except that she must have been even more beautiful when she was young than now.

"Do they have children, Nikki and Ted Haydn?"

"No, none."

"I've always thought you'd have liked children, Uncle Hugh."

He put his hand over hers. "You're my girl, Julia. You always have been."

"I know. I was thinking, when we first came in, that ever since Daddy was killed, you've been my father. I've felt you've been and that I could tell you anything. And then I wanted to ask you something, but couldn't—"

"What was it? If I can't answer, I'll say so."

"I wonder, what if you had married Nikki after all?"

"Oh, Julia, Julia, who can tell? I refuse to try to plumb the depths of the human heart, least of all my own."

CHAPTER

5

Frightened—never so frightened as now, on this mellow afternoon, golden as yesterday, the sky above the Greek Theatre an ineffable blue and the eucalyptus woods round about gently clattering long sickle leaves in a little breeze from the bay.

Julia peered from behind the curtain of one of the two small doors on either side of the Royal Door at center-back of the stage. She at once spotted Aunt Alex, extremely visible in a coral suit and large, tilted black hat, center and just far enough forward so as to hear well yet not be too aware of makeup. It's the effect one wants, she would say, not the crude details. She had Mr. de Rizzio on one side and Uncle Phil on the other, both listening with apparent respect while she waved an authoritative arm, no doubt telling of the presidents she had heard speak here, the great singers sing, the great actors and actresses act.

And her voice would be just loud enough, Julia knew, so that others before and behind might also be impressed by her fortunate experiences. Uncle Hugh was leaning back, and so were Mother and Mrs. de Rizzio and Greg. They'd heard it all before, more than once. As for Zoë de Rizzio, Aunt Alex had always amused her.

Hardly a seat vacant, Julia saw, all filled, right up to the heights, with the fond, proud, expectant families and friends of these no doubt wretched creatures (Julia hoped) wandering around behind her in really very good-looking costumes their mothers had whipped up on sewing machines. Julia's was purple with slashes of scarlet in the tight sleeves, puffed at the top, and in the long full skirt, fitted at the hips so that it flowed as she walked, with scarlet glimpsed and then hidden. A high collar lined with scarlet and wired to keep its shape rose at the back of her head. Celia was surprised, she said, at the success of her own efforts.

Julia had gazed at herself in the full-length mirror in Celia's closet door, filled her eyes with herself, could hardly have enough. *No* Portia or Ophelia or Cordelia or Juliet could possibly look more smashing (Aunt Alex's word) than she herself did at this moment. And when Uncle Hugh and Aunt Alex arrived in the big car, having picked up the de Rizzios on the way, she was the object of an explosion of admiring cries. Even Greg, never in his life given to compliments as to appearance ("You look like somebody's aunt," he'd told Leslie once when she did up her hair very becomingly and put on earrings), had to admit that in any case she wouldn't be a disgrace to them. "And I don't even have my full make-up on yet," she'd joyously reminded everyone. Mr. Winter's wife would take care of that when Julia got to the Greek Theatre.

But when she left the others at the entrance to go to find Mrs. Winter, she saw then that the Portias and Ophelias and Juliets and Cordelias and the one other Lady Macbeth were just as smashing as she, not to speak of the Othellos and Lears and Henry the Fifths. No one even looked at her twice—everyone was busy being made up and cracking jokes at each others' expense—until John spied her in the midst of the hubbub, raised an arm and waved, and came over. He took her hand in both of his, pressed it to his lips, and murmured in his usual dry tones, "My lady, you are magnificent!" then sat on the edge of a packing box and watched while Mrs. Winter made her up.

"John, are you scared?"

He answered, as if laughing at himself as always, that he was, that his boney knees were trembling, "and then I'm so thin that I look like a scarecrow in this outfit, with all my outlines revealed."

He exaggerated his thinness for fun, having, in a way, the same wry, dry, adult sense of humor that Greg had. Julia thought he looked extremely handsome in his stark black doublet and hose, the black contrasting with his blond hair; his nose was straight and fine and his face lean, just as Hamlet's should be. He had on a large silver medal on a chain as in the pictures of Hamlet, and a white pleated ruff around his neck. He'd known exactly what speech he was going to do and why, even though Mr. Winter argued for another. He was like that, sure of himself, of what he had in mind, whether he was scared at this moment or not. He had a voice like an organ, and when he'd rehearsed his lines for the Festival in Mr. Winter's class at school, you wondered what else he could possibly have to learn.

"But what do you have to be afraid *of*?" demanded Julia.

"God knows—I wish I did."

"If neither of you had icy hands or hollow stomachs," Mrs. Winter said, "I'd know we were in for a disaster." And having made up Julia's chorus, six of them, who were to stand in their gray veils, three on each side of her at a distance, to relate her first speech to her second, Mrs. Winter went away to join her husband down in front of the stage where he could hiss up promptings if need be, heaven forfend.

They were tenth on the program, which now began. Some few of the actors stumbled in their lines, some hesitated, one or two couldn't seem to project their voices, but most were depressingly good. The other Lady Macbeth, rather plump (Julia had always pictured her as lean and tense to a degree), threw herself into the "Out, damned spot" speech with enormous vigor, acting like fury, doing all those things Mr. Winter had forbidden Julia to do, lunging forward and back, grasping her head in despair, striking her chest, pointing off into the audience as if spying out the ghost of Banquo, and making her way offstage at the end as if dazed during her last cries of "To bed, to bed, to bed!" But she got a splendid hand; the audience loved all that heaving around, apparently. Therefore, thought Julia, they'll be insufferably bored with me. What if Mr. Winter had been completely wrong? She wished she could go home.

The thing was, said John, while everybody was congratulating the girl as she came backstage, flushed and triumphant over her success, that she hadn't enunciated clearly. The judges would have to give her zero on enunciation. "You've got a good strong voice, Julia. You can do all the things Mr. Winter wants, but if the judges can't hear every single word up there at the back of the theater, nothing else matters."

It was time for him to go on. He went out through the Royal Door and down to the front of the stage. He stood there for a moment in silence—quite a long moment— until there was a hush, almost a puzzled hush, all over the theater. Then he began in a quiet yet resonant voice that Julia knew was reaching every ear. You might have thought he *was* alone, so naturally did the words come from him. Never once, during his entire speech, did he let go of the audience, continually varying the color and emphasis of what he was saying. Without the least touch of melodrama, his voice gradually rose in power and volume to the lines where he calls his stepfather "bloody, bawdy villain! Remorseless, treacherous, lecherous, kindless villain!" Then, without losing force, yet quieting a little, he made his plans to trick this murderer into revealing himself, whereby Hamlet would "catch the conscience of the King."

Those were the last words; there was a breath of silence—then the applause was tremendous. Julia felt her arms ripple and the feathery shivers go around the back of her neck. Her throat tightened—there hadn't been applause like this for anyone else, nothing near it. What a triumph for Mr. Winter as well as for John. And John had turned away to leave the stage, but had to go back because the applause kept coming. When it finally, almost reluctantly died out, he came through the curtains and Julia, unable to speak, threw her arms around his neck, and he stood there laughing with his arms around her, then kissed her a good, sound kiss for happiness. She had to laugh in return to see the lipstick she'd left on his lips in a ridiculous smudge. Everyone came up while she tried to scrub it away; it seemed no one could be jealous of him. He was simply too good to be jealous of.

Now Julia stood at the parting of the curtains ready to make her own entrance, while the chorus went onstage through the side doors and arranged themselves. And just as she lifted the curtain, it came to her that she'd thought of something in the middle of the night: toward the end of her second speech, in the midst of exhorting Macbeth, there was a possible difficulty, a chance for some sort of confusion. But what was it? she wondered in desperation. The actual difficulty had completely escaped her—nothing was left but the knowledge that it had appeared to her very clearly. How could she have known then but not now!

No time to think—

She stood looking out over the innumerable faces and, in a split second of strange concentration, picked out Uncle Hugh in the sixth row center looking up at her, leaning forward a little, smiling with assured expectancy. She waited for the hush as John had done. Then, speaking at a measured pace, strongly and steadily, began

> Come you spirits
> That tend on mortal thoughts—

Adamant as stone, was in her mind behind the words as she spoke them. She no longer saw the audience but was taken up with listening to her own voice as she sent it out to that topmost row at the back of the theater.

In full command of herself, she felt her strength right to the end of the speech.

> Come, thick night,
> And pall thee in the dunnest smoke of hell,
> That my keen knife see not the wound it makes,
> Nor heaven peep through the blanket of the dark
> To cry "Hold, hold!"

The chorus began moving forward, there came a burst of applause, but the chorus held up their gray arms and the applause died away—there was to be more. Julia walked to the back of the stage, and while the chorus intoned what had occurred meanwhile, she turned and came slowly forward again, clasping her hands in anguish, rubbing them together. "Jangled in the mind—sick in the soul," Mr. Winter had said. "Groan out your 'Oh's' slowly, Julia, slowly—*wring* them out." Yes, but what had it been that had troubled her so in the middle of the night?

41

Yet here's a spot. . . . Out, damned spot! out, I say! One; two. Why then 'tis time to do't. Hell is murky. Fie, my lord, fie! a soldier, and afeard? What need we fear who knows it, when none can call our power to account? Yet [she peers sideways, to the right, to the left, hands spread as though pushing away the sight] who would have thought the old man to have had so much blood in him? . . . The Thane of Fife had a wife. Where is she now? What, will these hands ne'er be clean? No more o' that, my lord, no more o' that. You mar all with this starting. . . . Here's the smell of the blood still—wash your hands—

No, no! Not right—

Come, give me your hand—

No, oh, God!

Here's the smell of the blood still. All the perfumes of Arabia will not sweeten this little hand. Oh, oh, oh! . . . What, will these hands ne'er be clean?"

She stood silent, staring. The lines were scrambled, coming to her in the wrong order. She was lost: couldn't think, couldn't remember. Mr. Winter was whispering, whispering, but a cloud of crows had settled to the right of the theater, high in the eucalyptus trees, scolding in their harsh, prehistoric voices. Julia stood, her mind a nothingness. And she was cold, ice-cold at last, bone-cold, sick in her soul. She, not Lady Macbeth.

Mr. Winter—Mr. Winter—

CHAPTER

6

Here she was, still awake at midnight and absolutely incapable of anything but going over and over that terrible drive home from the Greek Theatre with Mother and Uncle Phil trying to comfort her (but Greg never saying a word) when she'd looked forward to nothing but praise because she'd known what she could do. She'd been terrified when she stepped onto the stage, but never once imagined she could fail. Miserably! Failed Mr. Winter. Failed Uncle Hugh, and he'd had nothing but compliments for what she'd done well.

"—but of course he was superb—com-pletely superb!" That was Aunt Alex when they got home, saying this as though the matter needed to be settled once and for all and she the only one who could do it. Meanwhile she was sailing into the dining room straight for Uncle Phil's chair at the head of the table. "I can't believe it, and

43

John's only your age—seventeen, did you say, Greg? I've never heard those lines delivered more impressively in my whole life, and I expect I've heard *every*one of *any* importance do Hamlet."

To which Greg piped up, cheery and friendly, "I think your place is over there, Aunt Alex," and pointed across to the chair opposite.

"Oh, but Greg, that would spoil the order," and she turned to Uncle Phil with what Julia and Greg called her "luv-ly" smile, as though naturally he would come and draw his chair out for her because she so hated to sit at the side. And like an idiot he did, and slid his chair gently in under her broad bottom and took her place at the side, which made Julia stonier than ever. Then down sank Aunt Alex, most graciously, as if she always sat at the head of the table, no matter who the host might be. And Mother said, "Well, Alex, and so you've made it, after all," because there'd been a little tussle between them last time and Celia had won.

"Oh, Celia, you know how I hate sitting between people or at some little old end place. I'm a big woman and I need room. And your Phil's such a sweetheart. He understands me, don't you, Phil?" She reached over and patted his hand and lifted her chin at him as if they shared some deep and special secret. Meanwhile, Uncle Phil had the most ridiculous, self-conscious look on his face and glanced over at Uncle Hugh, who seemed to be getting an enormous kick out of all this.

Then Aunt Alex got back to her subject again, because all that about John had really been about Julia: how she'd failed and disappointed everyone.

"I expect, Julia," she said, flinging out her napkin ahead of Celia as if she were the hostess and giving everyone permission to fling out theirs, "I expect you're quite taken with John Naismith. I know *I* should have been as a girl—oh, *mad* about him!" And she sent Julia that knowing look she had and her quick little wink that said that, no matter how anyone protested, she understood. And Julia wondered if Aunt Alex would have been as taken with John—"oh, *mad* about him!"—if she could have seen him every day at school in his worn cords, thin at the knees, and his old shoes and shapeless jacket that went up in the back, just himself, John, and not all gotten up as Hamlet in black and silver. She'd probably never even have noticed him.

Julia studied her with what she trusted was her distant look. Not angry, not cornered, but just cold and distant. However, it was boring she should bring up John in front of everyone because he *was* quite often on Julia's mind, and she was determined to be Juliet when Mr. Winter put on the play next term. There'd be no doubt as to who would be Romeo, so of course it would be a perfect experience.

"I like him well enough," she said indifferently, "but then I like most of the Shakespeare class."

"Like him well enough!" mocked Aunt Alex. She could just imagine, and she said Julia must have the glooms she'd been so quiet, but it was no use, because what's done can't be undone and the whole thing might just as well be forgotten.

At this, Mrs. de Rizzio leaned forward and began telling some of her experiences in the theater when she was in her twenties, getting bad notices but learning from them, getting devastating attacks of stage fright, but saying how you had to work through all this no matter what art you were involved in. Aunt Alex waved her hand and said she couldn't understand why Julia should be so concerned about getting confused this afternoon when, after all, she wasn't going to be an actress but a writer, or so she'd given everyone to understand.

"But I want all sorts of experience. The more I can get, the more to write about." And then Julia remembered something. "Oh, Aunt Alex, I forgot to tell you! You remember Oren Moore, Mrs. Moore's son—the famous pianist?"

Aunt Alex surveyed Julia without expression. "Well, of course. Naturally. What about him?"

"*Well,* he was at Mrs. Moore's house the other day, practicing and resting, all completely private—not a soul knew about it—before he went back to Ireland to get ready for his next tour. And he and Mrs. Moore made me do my Lady Macbeth for them—"

"Why, Julia," exclaimed Mrs. de Rizzio, her eyes shining, "i-*mag*-ine that! You did your lines for *him*—"

"Yes, and so then he asked me what he could do in return for my performance, which I must say I did as perfectly as it would be humanly possible for me to do it, remembering every single thing Mr. Winter had told me, and so I asked him if he'd play Mrs. Moore's last two pieces for me, the Greek ones, and it was *mar*velous." She shook her head, gazing at Aunt Alex. "You should have heard—just the three of us there by ourselves. I always remember Mrs. Moore composing them and then prac-

ticing them late at night when we lived at the de Rizzios',
and he said, after he was finished, that he wanted to tell
her how very much he admired them, and she said that
now she was out of her misery, because he'd neglected
before this to say anything. He was playing the Rach-
maninoff Concerto Number 3 when I came in." And Julia
closed her eyes for a second as if recalling that mighty
sound, rolling down the stairs and drowning her.

There was a little silence while Aunt Alex studied Julia
with the strangest expression on her face and Julia sat
there, smiling back at her "like a cat licking its chops after
a bowl of tuna," Celia said later. Then there was a buzz
of conversation about Oren Moore, and wasn't it true
he was coming back to the bay area for a concert later
on in the year? But Aunt Alex said not a single word,
and Julia slid Uncle Hugh a quick glance and he caught
it and then, with his elbows on the table and his cup
in both hands, smiled down into it with a certain little
smile.

And now finally, when the buzz had died away, "Well,
all *I* have to say is, what a very great pity, Julia," said Aunt
Alex, "that you couldn't have given *us* the pleasure of a
perfect performance instead of having to retire in such ab-
ject defeat to the embarrassment of us all." Now she rested her chin on one hand and turned and smiled at Uncle
Hugh, letting a moment pass before she started to speak
again. "However," she said, and there was a cutting
edge to her tone, "a person can do only so many things,
and some of them he might not do very well no matter
how long he tries."

47

She meant his art, not Julia's, and so there she was, laughing at him in front of everyone, as she had so many times, holding him up to ridicule, and the de Rizzios knew how Uncle Hugh loved his painting and would understand the mockery. Then she said that all this reminded her—and she was talking straight to Celia—that that Nikki Haydn was in San Francisco again. *There* was someone who'd wasted her life, trotting around all over the globe, marrying disastrously, getting divorced, and now trying to get Ted Haydn back—so *she'd* heard. "I always did think her harebrained," finished Aunt Alex, "a rubbishy, shallow little thing."

Julia's heart began going lippety-lip, and she sent Uncle Hugh a quick sideways glance, and there was that tightness at the corners of his eyes she knew so well, the tightness that meant he was hard-pressed or angry or hurt or humiliated. His face was flushed and his mouth set. And he said in a low voice, as if just to Aunt Alex, that he couldn't imagine why Nikki Haydn should be called harebrained and rubbishy simply because she chose to come back at last to where she had been born.

But now Celia, looking perfectly furious, her eyes sparking, said that Nikki was neither harebrained nor rubbishy, that the two of them had been writing each other for years, back and forth, and that Nikki happened to be a splendid person and a great friend of hers. Over her clasped hands she stared right at Aunt Alex, and her eyes never left Aunt Alex's the whole time she was speaking.

Aunt Alex stared back for a second or two, obviously

astounded. Then she turned to Uncle Hugh again. "Well, well," she said, "the little artistic circle. How charming! No wonder Hugh enjoys his art school, and always insists on never, never missing a single Saturday."

Now Greg, dependable old Greg, because he must have felt everything heating up to a crisis and far too much being said for Uncle Hugh's good, all at once put in that he'd been looking at *Macbeth*, puzzling why Julia had gotten muddled, and he thought he'd solved the mystery. He had an idea it was the number of times "hands" was repeated in those last lines of Lady Macbeth's sleepwalking scene, and out of his back pocket he took one of their small red leather-bound volumes of the plays with *Macbeth* in it. "Will these hands ne'er be clean?" and then "all the perfumes of Arabia will not sweeten this little hand," and then right in the next line, "Wash your hands, put on your nightgown," and then the last time, "—come, give me your hand. What's done cannot be undone. To bed, to bed, to bed."

Yes, yes, of course that was it, what had been eating away at Julia in the middle of the night. Something had been trying to warn her, trying to tell her to pay attention! Mr. de Rizzio clapped and said that Greg had always been a detective, running down clues and getting the answers. He should *be* one.

But Aunt Alex, a bright red spot in either cheek, said coldly that, indeed, Greg was the clever one. Hadn't she always said so? But in point of fact, who on *earth* at the Greek Theatre, among all those doting mamas and papas and grannies and grandpas, up there only to listen to their own pets and who'd never read a page of Shakespeare in their lives or ever seen a single one of his plays, would have guessed that Julia had ruined her chance? It was all much ado about nothing, and she looked completely bored and fed up.

Had Aunt Alex, then, ever read a page of Shakespeare in her life? What she loved was a good murder mystery and a box of dark chocolates, all cozy in her downy bed late at night.

When they were clearing up the dishes and putting everything away, Greg and Julia and Celia and Uncle Phil, they had to laugh all over again at the memory of Aunt Alex's expression when she was listening to Julia's story about Oren Moore.

"But who would ever have guessed," said Uncle Phil, "that Julia's story would lead to Alex humiliating Hugh again, when that would be the last thing Julia would have wanted!"

"And why haven't you ever told me, Mother, that you and Nikki have been friends and writing each other all these years?"

"But you don't even know her, Julia, and never have."

"Well, I remember perfectly well being told when I was little that Aunt Alex got Uncle Hugh away from Nikki, and as it happens I met her over at the art school yesterday morning."

"Did you, now! But I don't tell you everything, any more than you tell me. Especially these days, I can imagine, very little."

No, thought Julia, even though we love each other. And she thought, too, as she stood there wiping and wiping one dish while the others went on about something else, how in families, everyone living close together, so much isn't told—Greg down in his cave writing to Leslie, Mother and Uncle Phil together, and herself writing in her *Book of Strangenesses*. We live in the globes of our own private worlds, she thought, and sometimes they merge—but still there's the separateness. And she'd long gotten over thinking she owned Celia, the way she used to feel when they were at the de Rizzios' and she'd told herself she hated her mother for wanting someone besides her children.

CHAPTER

7

October 25

Now it's half past three. I didn't get to sleep until after one and here I am, wide-awake again.

What I must write down is the dream I've just had—exactly, while I still remember it, get back the exact details, my feeling of someone here when I woke up, a special someone, and that I've had this dream before, the most terrible one of my life and so real, as if it had actually happened.

What I don't understand is that I felt much younger than I am now. I was very young and the feeling of loneliness was awful. I was by myself walking up along the streets we always took, Daddy and I, when he was through writing, and sometimes Mother if she wasn't busy, up into the hills along the usual path. And it was almost as if I had it in mind to meet someone—but who? I almost felt I knew, perhaps from some other dream.

And now I was on the trail, hurrying, not paying much attention to my whereabouts because I was so familiar with this path. Then I happened to look up, troubled because the trees, the oaks and eucalyptus, were getting sparse when they should have been thickening into the woods of pines and manzanita. And I was shocked to the pit of my stomach to see that not only were there no trees ahead, but that out there, where the woods should have been, falling away from Berkeley with the bay and San Francisco and the Golden Gate and Marin County beyond, there was nothing but bare hills. Brown, empty, barren hills going on forever like an infinity of brown breasts. I was alone in a waste of these barren hills and I could see no end to them no matter which way I turned. Berkeley was gone, and the bay and the city. Everything.

In that moment I knew that there was no one anywhere to tell me the way, to explain to me what had gone wrong, what horrible chance had brought me to this wilderness of nothingness, and knew that I might wander forever where I could see no paths and would never come to anything, to any house or any person who could lead me home. I had a feeling I didn't any longer have a home, no mother and father, no Greg. There were no birds, no small animals. There was nothing but complete silence, not the least stir of wind or breeze. The sun was shining—or was it? Everything seemed neutral like the color of the hills, not the rich golden brown scattered with live oaks I know so well when summer has come, but a dead, neutral brown. And the light was neutral, neither sunny nor gray. It seemed no particular time of day, not especially morning or evening or afternoon.

It was as if I were the only person in the world, a small child and completely alone. I called until I was hoarse, and I was sobbing so hard I couldn't speak another word. But there was no answer and I knew there never would be one. Nothing. I ran on shaking legs up one hill and over and down the next, but nothing ever changed no matter which way I went. And the strangest thing was that I felt I had been here before, running like this in anguished desperation, but in that other time I had been with someone, at least coming up through those trees I knew so well that had now vanished.

I sank down and lay curled on my right side with my face hidden in the short, rough, dead-looking growth because my legs wouldn't any longer hold me. I couldn't go on, and besides, there would have been no point. And then, because I was utterly defeated, I suppose, utterly desolate, I woke up.

My heart was jolting with terror exactly as if this dream had been real. My whole body was damp and my throat ached as if I'd been crying for hours. I thought of Daddy— but *why*? Immediately on waking I had a sense of his presence and it was so strong that I almost felt that if I got up and went padding through the house I might find him, perhaps sitting all by himself in the dark in the living room. But he's been dead for almost nine years! Why should I feel this? There would be no use going through the house in the dark, hunting for him. I lay there remembering how it had been when we lost him.

I would *not* believe his plane had gone down. Uncle Hugh tried to convince me as best he could, but I struck out at him and sobbed, "No, no—he *will* come back, he *will*—he's *not* dead! I *know*—I know exactly what happened." When I found out that being a pilot meant that he would fly for miles in the dark across water from one country to another and that his plane could be shot down and that he would fall through the black sky and be killed, I had it all fixed in my mind so that I needn't worry. I told myself, and saw in my imagination that he would fall into a forest and that the trees would break his fall and save him as if they would hold out their branches to receive him.

I remember Greg later on staring at Mama (you see, I'm calling her that because I'm back being six again), his face very white and set, and saying "What was the use anyway—what was the *use* of him being killed?" and Mama said that after this there wouldn't be any more wars, that that was why the war had been fought, so that the world would be safe from them. But Greg said, "I don't believe it—I don't be*lieve* it—how can anybody *say* that, how can they know?" And he slammed off into his room and there was silence while the door kept on being closed and I was sure he was crying and didn't want us to see him, but Mama and I cried together. I made her say that maybe Daddy would be found and brought back—couldn't he— *couldn't* he be? I don't remember what she said, but of course he never was.

Now all at once, lying there in the dark after my dream and thinking so strongly about him, I saw him in his plane with the night sky around him. It was so real and yet I was awake but with my eyes closed. I was with him in the plane, felt when it was hit and knew wrenchingly how he must have felt, knowing that it was going down and that he would never see us again. Mama was there in his mind's eye, Mama sitting at her dressing table while he brushed and brushed her long glossy hair, then lifted it and kissed the back of her neck, and afterwards they'd snuggle down in bed together spooned in close to each other. What was it they used to sing?

> And we'll cling together like the i-ivy
> On the old ga-ar-den wall—

And there was me in the hot golden berry garden in back of the little brown shingled bungalow where we lived then, with the sun pouring down and making the perfume of the blackberries stronger than ever and Greg and Bob playing next door with their old streetcar stuff, and Patchy-cat and me lying on the little closed-in space of thick grass that smelled so good when you burrowed your nose into it and I'd be telling Patchy-cat and the Japanese dolls Continued Stories. And Daddy would know that now he'd never have a chance to find out if his story would ever be accepted and whether he could have gone on writing when he got back and be published. His last story was his best, he knew that, but no one else ever would. Unless somehow Mama would think to go through all the papers he'd packed up before he left.

There it all was in his mind when he knew he was lost, everything at once, and then the burning pieces of the plane falling around him—and then the crash of impact—and nothing more.

Was that the way it was, our being with him, Mama and Greg and me? I will write a story about him—in memory of him, the only thing I can do for him. I feel it so alive in my mind, see it so vividly, as if it had actually happened that way, so that surely I can write this story even though it's like nothing I've ever tried before. I'm frightened of it, frightened I'll find I'm not worthy to write it. But I'm going to try.

But one thing I know—I'm happy, having in my mind what I'm going to write next, frightened or not. It's such rich material (Mr. Winter's words when he comes across some good writing full of feeling). I don't care at all now that I failed yesterday, except for Mr. Winter's sake—I care for his!—and that I have to face everybody at school, and Fran. That Fran Brinkley, always irritating me, always trying to get the better of me in one way or another—and why, for the love of heaven, why me?—and yet, yes, fascinating me, her and her college men who take her over to the city for dancing at the St. Francis, and then she'll have a crying session on the ferry coming home and her college man (whichever one it is at the time) will tenderly wipe away the rivulets of mascara! She seems to me turned toward sex like a sunflower toward the sun. But now I couldn't care less about Fran. I have this story to write.

CHAPTER

8

Fran came out of the cubicle pulling down her sweater and straightening her skirt. Without a word she came over to the washbasins, put her black patent leather purse on the shelf below the mirror, opened it, scoured around amongst the tumult inside, which seemed to include a number of smudged and crumpled letters, found her lipstick, and began smoothing it onto her full lips, pulling her upper lip down to make it taut, and crinkling her lower one. Julia silently involved herself in combing her hair, giving a good deal of attention to the parting and being amused at Fran's comical-looking upper lip. Now Fran tossed the lipstick into her purse and drew out her comb.

"Well, Julia," she said briskly all at once, "and how's the family? Any news yet?"

Julia immediately understood and a flush of intense

resentment swept through her body as though a tide had rushed in. "What do you mean by that?"

"Oh, you know. Any little brother or sister coming along?"

"I can't see that it's any of your business. Why you're so interested in my family, I can't imagine."

"Well!" said Fran, pursing her lips with amusement, "How angry we get—" and she sounded exactly like Aunt Alex calling Julia a little wet hen. Fran shot up her eyebrows, carefully plucked into thin crescents, and proceeded to comb down, smooth as smooth, her shining mouse brown bobbed hair, cut into bangs across her forehead and precisely to the lobes of her ears, from which swung long earrings. She lifted her shoulders and tilted her head. "I only thought you'd find it fun, having a new little baby to help take care of, being more the domestic type, though lord knows *I* wouldn't. But when women marry again they always want babies by their new husbands."

More the domestic type! Well, there was to be no baby, Celia being too old. All the same, Fran's words left a faint stain of anxiety and an indefinable depression. No doubt as they were supposed to have done.

Fran went on combing, leaning forward to examine her face minutely from time to time. Then she put the comb away, drew out a little case of mascara and began applying the brush, tilting her head back to flick the brush neatly and surely along her upper lashes. Out of the sides of her eyes Julia watched the slender fingers, tapered slightly at the sides just below the pink, perfectly kept nails, delicately at work. Why the idea of delicacy should have surprised her, she wasn't sure, except that Fran, in herself, seemed anything but delicate. Julia had never failed to be fascinated by the movements of Fran's hands, and by the way she seemed always at home in her clothes, as if they must feel beautifully right and she was pleased with herself and their rightness.

"Isn't it a kick," said Fran, "the way Mrs. Winter follows that little Mr. Winter around as if she positively worships him. Honestly! Can you even so much as imagine what she sees in that funny little monkey of a man, with his wisps of hair standing on end and the way he works his jaw around when he gets excited? He kills me. And he dotes on her—well, that isn't surprising. Isn't he the lucky one to have a young thing like that! But why in the name of heaven did she marry him? I've never been able to make it out."

Julia studied her coldly in the mirror for a moment. "You wouldn't know," she said finally. "You wouldn't know anything about the Winters because you've never been to rehearsals at their house or to one of their parties and seen the way they are with each other—" She'd been going to go on, but now she fell silent, finding herself all at once unwilling to confess what she felt about those two—what she felt about their consideration for one another, their appreciation of what each had to offer—to such a one as Fran Brinkley. Julia turned back to her own image, opened her compact and powdered her nose, full of scornful disgust.

"Oh, well, I probably will be—at their rehearsals and

parties, I mean." Fran watched herself as she lifted her chin, brought her lips forward a little, and ran a hand caressingly over her cheek. "Then I can behold for myself this marvel of marriage. Such a privilege! As we're all practically certain that John'll get Romeo next term, I decided to sign up and try out for Juliet. I thought it'd be rather a lark playing opposite him."

Never had it entered Julia's mind that Fran Brinkley would be in the least interested in Mr. Winter's class, wholly absorbed as she seemed to be in the life of dances and new clothes and going out with her college men.

At once, all Julia's joyful looking forward to the Shakespeare class next spring and those hours spent at the Winters' house fell into ruin. Fran there! Fran in class, of course winning the part of Juliet and therefore, along with John, being the center. But Fran as Juliet! Suddenly the idea struck Julia as being so incongruous she had to put down her comb and stare at Fran in the mirror. "Of course," she said, "there's always the horrid possibility you might not get the part. Juliet was thirteen. Could you act the part of a child?"

Fran didn't even trouble to look at Julia but smiled to herself, packed up everything in her purse and snapped it closed with a final, firm click. "That particular child, yes. I usually get what I'm after, if I want it hard enough. Did you have the idea of trying out for Juliet yourself? Of course, some people have a gift for memorizing lines and some don't. I've always found I do—no trouble at all. Which reminds me: sorry about the Greek Theatre." And she went over to the door of the rest room and stood there, looking back, half in, half out, with that slight, assured smile still on her lips.

"You know perfectly well, Fran Brinkley, that you were absolutely delighted."

Fran gave her typical pleased little chuckle deep in her throat and the door whuffed closed behind her.

October 27

I keep trying to begin my story and getting it all wrong and my stomach burns. I thought that if Fran gets Juliet it won't matter because I have my own work to do, but if I haven't that, I'm nowhere. I've only got my life the way it is.

Now I'm going to start again calmly and not in a state of nerves, because I respect this story so much.

"He is alone—he has set out, and recognizes once again his companion fear, that he is aware of each night after he has gotten his plane up and started across the Channel."

But right away I run into trouble in my first sentence. I say he is alone but that he has a companion. So maybe I should put it the other way around.

"He has set out alone, yet now recognizes once again his faithful companion fear, that he is aware of each night after he has gotten his plane up and started across the Channel. A hollow of dark terror lies ahead, soon to be crisscrossed by lances of gunfire, and he must enter it."

I like this better and maybe now I can go on, about his having the knowledge, down underneath his constant, tense watchfulness for the first enemy plane, of how much he'd wanted some place out in the country and to give up his insufferably boring job at the calculating machine company so that he could just write, and perhaps raise chickens and sell their eggs and maybe fruit from the trees.

So Daddy, just a few months before leaving for camp when he didn't know he was going to be called up, put that little bit of money he'd inherited from his aunt into a small farm because it was such a beautiful piece of land and he loved it. He did it on an irresistible impulse without telling Mother, he wanted it so badly and thought he could persuade her when she saw it that it was right for all of us. But she didn't agree and was sick he hadn't saved the money so that when the owner of our bungalow got ready to sell, we could buy it. It was the only really serious quarrel they'd ever had, and Greg and I didn't know a thing about it, they kept it so carefully between them.

And when Daddy went away, he had to leave her with the payments to make because he couldn't sell the farm with all the husbands being called up and everyone uncertain, so that he's been overcome with guilt ever since. It's hung in his mind, he's gone over and over it. He's thinking of us and how we used to go climbing up in the hills— Oh, could that be what brought him so close to me after my dream? How I was up there without him and he was gone forever and I'd never walk with him in the hills again? And now I have the strangest feeling about that dream. I know there's another behind it, or some memory of Daddy and me back when I was six. I can't get it, but it's there—it's *there*. Perhaps if I leave it, it'll come to me. And does he have the strongest feeling that this will be his last flight?

CHAPTER

9

Julia, sitting on the edge of her bed with the door closed because one of her letters had Oren Moore up in the corner of the envelope with his Irish address, let her hands with his letter sink to her lap while she wondered why on earth he would write to her. She had a pair of scissors and now very carefully cut along the top.

November 15

Dear Julia—

Ever since Mother and I have been back here at Moorelands I've been thinking about you and wanting to write. Every day, of course, I do nothing but get ready for the tour and a good many evenings are filled with friends or we go out. But the ones we like best are spent dreaming like cats by the fire. After I've finished working we often walk out across the moors for an hour before

64

dinner, something I need after sitting at the piano for so long.

This is such beautiful country, Julia, that I'd like you to see it and wish you could come over with my mother one of these days. I often think of a young girl standing by the grand piano being Lady Macbeth. And now you'll be Juliet, at least so she says. She hasn't any doubt. Then there's your writing, which I gather is of the greatest importance to you. If it is, your life will be scattered with disappointments and frustrations as mine has been. It usually is when you want passionately to do good work. But there'll be successes, all the more satisfying by contrast with the disappointments, even humiliations, which are so hard to swallow. I wish those judges could have seen you do Lady Macbeth as I did.

And now I'm about to launch out again, and so will you before long. I'll think of you. I won't write, not even a postcard. No use promising what I won't do. But you'll be in my mind.

Good fortune!

Oren Moore

The cats, who had been asleep on Julia's bed, stretched and made small questioning sounds in their throats, and she felt their hard little feet pushing against her back. But for once she couldn't respond with a thorough, loving nuzzle into their warm fur. She was stunned. Oren had been moved to write her this long letter. He'd been thinking of her, he wanted her to come to his home with Rhiannon. But why? He'd often thought of her standing by Rhiannon's piano being Lady Macbeth, and knew about "wanting passionately to do good work." Well, at least *that* was it, exactly, "wanting passionately." But going over to Ireland with Rhiannon, that was ridiculous! Where was she supposed to get the money? And why would he want to see someone like herself when he knew all those beautiful, sophisticated women? Even famous ones, no doubt. Actresses, and people like that.

After reading his letter again, and then, even, once again, she folded it and returned it to its envelope. She understood. He'd been thinking about ruffling her hair as if she'd been an infant. He'd seen how furious it made her even though he'd given no sign but just turned back to the piano. And what he was doing now was saying he was sorry.

She picked up another letter, this one from Rhiannon.

November 16

Dearest Julia:

Your last letter reached me yesterday, and I can only write you a quick one now because I must help Oren pack and get ready for London. But I have to tell you that I'm excited for you, to think you've actually finished your story, at least the first draft and that you like it better than anything you've ever done because it's more real! By now you'll have finished the final draft so that you'll have it ready for me to read when I get home.

That will be December 6 as I see it now unless I decide to stay in New York for a day or two to visit friends. I have so much to tell you, about visiting my Willie Yeats at his stone tower with its winding stairs, meaning for him the poet's difficult climb toward his vision, what he calls "the dreaming wisdom," and he took me up to the huge bare room at the top where butterflies get in and die against the panes. It was evening and there was brilliant moonlight across the floor.

It frightened me, going to see him—I can't tell you how frightened I was, he's become such a Personage, and then to come under those studying eyes that can put you at such a distance when they don't approve of something you've said or done. But I needn't have been frightened. We took up just where we left off when we were last together. I wore my medallion he gave me and he put out a finger to touch it but never said a word—only smiled. He didn't need to speak. We understood.

He says I haven't changed, but Julia, I looked at myself in the mirror afterwards in great excitement and then was in despair. Once it was said of me that I was beautiful, but no longer. I simply am not.

You must come down from your hilltop the next day after I get back. Oren and I will be setting off for London tomorrow morning, where he's to appear at the Royal Albert Hall the next night for the first performance of his tour. He's written you a letter which he's asked me to mail along with this one so you'll be getting both at the same time. Naturally I haven't read his—*vie privée!*

My love to you—we'll talk for hours!
Rhiannon

Julia sat for some two or three minutes staring gravely into space and absently stroking and stroking the cats, who were trying to get into her lap. Well, but what does *"vie privée"* mean? And how do you say it? Vy priv-*ee* or vy *priv*-ee? Uncle Hugh—I'll ask him. He knows French.

She picked up the third letter.

November 15

Dear Julia:

Well, of course I want to read your story. After all, I'm your closest friend. But I understand your still wanting to think about it before you send it off, even though you're pleased with it. How does a person ever get to the end of wanting to make changes!

You've said you envy me being in Paris with so many things to see and do, and having the experience of living here and going to school and getting used to speaking French. I'm still not very good at it—or at least, I mean I can't get that *r* to roll in the back of my throat, sort of juicy and gargling, the way they do it, and my dad. He has practically no American accent at all, he's been over so often, and everyone says my mother's is "tr-r-rès charmant." But no one ever says anything about mine!

Julia, to tell you the truth, I get homesick. I get homesick to hear my own language again. I've made friends and even have a boyfriend, but you and Greg come first. I miss his silly old jokes. He's really a very comical individual, coming up with those incredible puns of his. The strangest thing is that one slight, casual little scene, the memory of it, brings on the homesickness. You won't believe it, but it's of Greg pulling down his glasses and peering at me over them, very solemnly, Professor Cranley, then suddenly pushing them up again and grinning at me.

I want to see Nefertiti on top of his desk, gazing into the past with her lovely chin up so that her head, with its tall headdress, is slightly tilted back on that long, smooth neck, and what can she possibly have been looking at all these centuries? Some lost Egyptian scene that seems to give her a calm, deep satisfaction of the soul. Now all at once I have an idea for a poem—Nefertiti, and Greg's room, and homesickness, and his looking at me over his glasses, his special personality. Well, but now I've muddied the idea, or perhaps confused it, of my remembrance of Nefertiti, just herself. That's one poem, pure and single.

So then, quartet. Four poems, belonging together. Yes, "Quartet for a Certain Young Man." That's it—that's it. I can almost see them on the page. *But don't tell Greg*—I'll send them to him for Christmas, but it's so close I must get to work at once. Write me! But then you always do. And Rhiannon will be home soon and you must tell me everything, and about Oren—if there's any news of him. And about John. Will you be Juliet opposite him?

Love—of course
Leslie

Julia flopped back on the bed with Leslie's letter clasped to her chest, and the cats climbed onto her stomach where they tried, both at once, to settle. But as Sandy was bulkier and stronger than Gretchy, he easily shoul-

69

dered her to one side and curled down, with his tail waving across Julia's face before he wrapped it around himself, and Gretchy came and pushed in close against her neck.

"Hello, my Gretchy," murmured Julia, and began scratching behind her ears and all over her face, which sent her into such a dither of ecstasy that she got herself right up under Julia's chin, at least her top part, so that Julia shouldn't neglect her for an instant. But, "Uncle Hugh!"— Julia dumped the cats and was away into the hall to the phone.

It rang and rang until Hulda answered, so that she must have been getting dinner with her hands all floury and having to be rubbed together and wiped off, because she sounded rather pressed.

"Tait residence," she announced, breathless but dignified, and you couldn't have quite put your finger on the intonation revealing her Swedishness.

"Oh, Hulda—hello, it's me. Are you all right?"

"Julia. Yes, but I'm hot. There's an enormous dinner party tonight and, oh, the dishes your Aunt Alex expects me to fix. Well, there, now—I'll hang up—there's your—"

"Uncle Hugh—"

"Hullo, how's my girl?"

"Fine. A dinner party tonight, I hear."

"Worse luck," he groaned. "But I have to put up with them occasionally, Alex says, and people'll stay and stay, and I'll have to play bridge, horrible thought. *In*-finitely teedjus."

"Uncle Hugh, you speak French, don't you?"

70

"Well, you could hardly call it that, but I get along—barely."

"What's 'vy privee'?"

"*Vy privee?*" He thought it over. "Vy privee. Oh, could you possibly mean *'vie privée'*?" He said it "vee preevay." "If you do, it means 'private life.' Does that fit in? Does it make sense?"

"Yes—yes, it does. I've had a letter from Rhiannon Moore, and she said that. It has something to do with my letter from Oren Moore."

"Her *son*? *He's* written you?"

"Well, yes—a very nice letter, and I know why. But you're not to tell anyone."

"You mean not tell anybody about the letter, or not tell anybody that you know why he wrote it? Naturally, I won't say a word, but still—"

"I said it's a perfectly nice letter, but *vie privée!*"

"Ah, yes, well, of course. And what does Mrs. Moore have to say?"

"All about having dinner with someone special after years and years of not seeing him. But I'll tell you when we get together. I haven't seen you for ages, not since my disaster, so when shall we plan? Next Saturday?"

"Or maybe a week from then," said Uncle Hugh. "In the afternoon?"

"But we could have lunch together at the usual place when we go to the park. I have to get some Christmas presents and I don't have to go over to the city, but it would be fun, and I could meet you at Buscaglia's and whoever gets there first will save a table."

71

There was a short silence at the other end, then Uncle Hugh said consideringly, "Well, I don't see why not. Yes, let's do that. I'd love to see you. A week from Saturday then, at Buscaglia's. Say at one o'clock—no, one thirty?"

"One *thirty*! I'll be perished by then. But, no, that's all right, because it'll give me plenty of time to shop. Good!"

As Julia hung up, it occurred to her that she'd be at Rhiannon's the next day after being with Uncle Hugh. She went to her room and studied the calendar on her desk. Why, no, it would be this Sunday Rhiannon would be home. The end of this week, she thought, not next. And I can take my story and read it to her. And shall I take Oren's letter because I'll bet she'd like to read it? But, no, he didn't give it to her. I think I'll keep it to myself, even from Uncle Hugh—imagine! My first letter from a famous person.

CHAPTER

10

It was what she meant about strangenesses constantly happening, turning a corner and running into something you couldn't possibly have imagined.

Julia went to Rhiannon's on Sunday, and there was Zoë de Rizzio out in her back garden with a bundle of soiled newspapers in her tiny reddened hands, and her feet pointing out in a V in their minute, fancy, high-heeled slippers, standing as she'd been taught to as a young girl.

"Rhiannon won't be back for several days after all, dearie. She dropped me a card—but come on in with me and have something to eat. I'm ready for it after cleaning out this aviary."

Now Zoë was pouring out the coffee while they waited for the bread to toast, and Julia lifted her cup in both hands and began to feel the way she used to, coming in here— comforted after the disappointment of not being able to read her story to Rhiannon.

"—but before I married Frank," Zoe was saying, "I was terribly in love with a young actor, Stephen Morgan, my first love. We were in several plays together and I thought for sure that— Oh, confound! Oh, drat! Julia, quick, crouch down." Zoë's wiry hand clutched at her and pulled. "Get yourself into the back bedroom." And with astonishing speed the little woman, hunched below window level, did as she'd directed Julia, and Julia, astounded, hunched her own self and followed.

"But what *is* it, what's happened? Who are we hiding from?"

They were in the bedroom, a shadowed room on the bushy side of the house where no one ever came, the room that used to be Greg's, where he'd lived in a mess as long as Celia could endure it, then she'd burst in and he'd be made to stir around at once and, groaning and complaining bitterly, try for some sort of order. Now it was depressingly neat and cold and quite dark at this time of the afternoon. Julia and Zoë stood just inside the door listening.

"Lydia Dormody," said Zoë in Julia's ear. "Rhiannon's sister. She's up to no good. She wants something or she'd never have come, and it has to do with minding Rhiannon's business, you can bet on that. Heaven knows *what* I'll be forced to say if I have to give in. It's all too exhausting."

After prolonged rings at the front doorbell, there was scrunching of the gravel along the driveway under the breakfast room windows. Presently the back door slammed, there were heel taps along the hall leading from the little back kitchen where Celia used to cook, and then a knock at the de Rizzios' kitchen door.

"Whoo-hoo, Zoë, it's just me, Lydia. Can I come in?"

"She's like Fate, relentless. Quick, Julia, get into the bathroom and flush the toilet, and I'll come out as if I've been changing the bed. It's no use—she'll barge right on in."

And so she did. Zoë went out to face her and Julia, a moment later, after flushing the toilet, could hear them talking. She went into the kitchen and Lydia Dormody stopped, turned, and looked at her with a hard, level look. Without greeting, she turned coolly back to Zoë and went on with what she'd been saying. Not a word had she had, not even so much as a card from Rhiannon about staying longer, and you'd think, wouldn't you, that one's own sister could at least take the trouble, not more than five minutes at most, *if* that, to scratch off a line!

Lydia had seated herself at the kitchen table and Zoë was pouring her a cup of coffee and putting another slice of bread into the toaster. Julia sat down near the Franklin stove and gazed at Lydia. Why, she—Lydia—hated her! That stare had been full of an intense resentment. But, why? What had she done?

"Now, what I want to know, Zoë, is if you have a key to that house? Surely you must have, living right here next door and keeping an eye on the place."

"But I *don't* have a key," and Zoë sat down and began stirring her coffee with little quick, annoyed clicks of her spoon against the side of the cup. "Julia, come and finish your toast—it'll get cold. I'd been cleaning out the aviary when Julia came, and we felt like having something to- gether. We've been sitting here talking—" At this, Lydia shot another hard glance at Julia, and Julia, going to the table, got the distinct idea that Zoë de Rizzio, considering Lydia's uninvited entrance, was now purposely needling her. They *had* heard the front doorbell but hadn't chosen to answer, was what she was saying.

"Well, that seems a strange thing," said Lydia, spread- ing plum jam thickly on her buttered toast and taking large, slow, appreciative bites with her big white teeth. Nobody else had damson plums around here, there weren't many on the tree, and nobody could make jam like Zoë. She'll eat it all up, thought Julia morosely, and sat watching Lydia, who was now ready for another piece of toast.

It was puzzling. Lydia Dormody—younger than her sister but with a white, drawn face, long flyaway black hair pulled loosely back into a careless knot, and Rhiannon's dark eyes, but Lydia's sunk in their sockets from which they peered out sharply like a watchful hawk's—had never had anything to do with Julia. So why this brooding dis- like?

"I certainly don't understand why you wouldn't have a key, Zoë, in case anything should happen like a fire or a burglary or something. And I can't understand for the life of me why Rhiannon didn't leave *me* a key. Now, *I* always think—"

"Why don't you ask her lawyer?" interrupted Zoë sharp- ly. "No doubt he has one."

"Oh, of course I did ask him, but he said Rhiannon had given strict orders to give it to no one, and he had no intention of doing so—not even to me!" cried Lydia, outraged. "Her very own sister. And was quite stubborn about it and, I thought, extremely rude to me. He seemed to have very little time, and I particularly wanted to talk to him about that medallion of hers. Why she keeps such a priceless thing as that in the house rather than in a safety deposit box at the bank, I can't imagine. She wears it just as if she'd gotten it at a department store. But she's always been childishly irresponsible about treasures—"

"Well, you don't have to worry about it," said Julia in a low voice, all at once seeing Rhiannon, and Mr. Yeats reaching out a finger to touch it. "She took it with her and wore it to dinner at her friend's house—you know, her poet's—and he just looked at it and then at her, and never said a word. Rhiannon wrote me." Julia had been looking down, contemplating the scene in her mind—it was so romantic, after all these years, and poignant, somehow. But now she lifted her eyes and met Lydia's black, blazing glare.

"Why, what do you mean, you impudent young one, you," breathed Lydia, "calling my sister by her first name. The nerve of you! Never let me hear you do such a thing again—"

All at once the devil possessed Julia. If the gauntlet had been thrown down, she'd pick it up. "Oh, but I don't see why I shouldn't, Miss Dormody. After all, Mrs. Moore asked me to, and it would have been rude not to. I've always called her Mrs. Moore, but she said that no close friend of hers was going to go on year after year calling her that. She wanted me to call her Rhiannon, and so in my letters I do. That was the day I was over there," went on Julia with seeming innocence, "when Oren was with her—staying with her—just before they left, and they made me do my Lady Macbeth speeches, and Oren asked me what he could do in return. So I asked him to play Rhiannon's last two pieces she's composed. I told him how much I liked it that he doesn't work himself around on the piano bench while he plays the way a lot of pianists do—you know, bending way down over the keys, then swaying far back with their eyes closed, and he and Rhiannon laughed and laughed because a friend of theirs does exactly that." Julia sat there smiling at Lydia, who had become a white-faced image of fury and who, plainly, could have reached across and struck her.

Now, suddenly, Zoë de Rizzio, as if picturing one of those soulful pianists, herself let out a sharp little bark of laughter, while Caruso the canary, in the same instant, burst into deafening song directly over Lydia Dormody's head. At this, dramatically, Lydia threw up her arms, then put her head down with her hands over her ears.

"How can you *endure* it, Zoë, this racket in the kitchen, this mechanical carrying on, and the constant scratching and seed-tossing and cheeping. It drives me mad—absolutely mad!" Now she pushed her chair back and picked up her purse. "As for you, young lady, I positively forbid you to call either my sister or her son by their first names. I am astonished that your mother has never impressed upon you the respect children are required to show their elders, especially to such people as my sister's son, a man known all over the world for his giftedness and accomplishments, who has played before presidents and kings. I can't *tell* you how *shocked* and *appalled* I am by your

78

presumption. Oren, in*deed*. And I am shocked at you as well, Zoë de Rizzio, joining in on the laughter."

With these words Lydia Dormody took herself out of the kitchen and into the front hall, opened the door and left, closing it behind her with a bang.

Julia and Zoë did not move, as if the last impressive scene of a play had been acted and the two halves of the curtain had flung themselves together across the stage.

"My word," said Zoë. "All that's needed is for Lydia to make a reentrance and stand and bow and hold out her hands, exhausted with gratitude for the applause, but unable to smile because she's still so shaken by the shattering demands of her art. Oh, my—there's a soul-eating going on inside Lydia, and it must go way, way back to childhood, perhaps, or possibly to Mr. Yeats. Well, at any rate, it's something I've never asked Rhiannon about." Zoë held her cup in her little crooked hands, took a sip or two of coffee, and reflected. "But one thing I'd say," she went on after a moment, "is that you seem to have an enemy in Lydia Dormody, and did before ever she knew you called Rhiannon and Oren Moore by their first names. I saw the way she looked at you when you came in and I wondered. There's a strange fierceness there. But why?"

"I don't know," said Julia. "But I do know that I have two enemies now, Miss Dormody and Fran Brinkley—only Fran's a smiling one. She's determined to get Juliet. We try out next Thursday so we'll have been chosen for our parts and will be all set to begin rehearsing by the time spring term begins."

"And you're ready to try out?"

"Not really, but I have three days, and actually I know the words—"

"Which isn't enough, is it? What scene have you chosen?"

"I want a very dramatic scene for my own choice, which we can have if we like, but each of us—that is, the girls—must do the one where Juliet's in the orchard waiting for her nurse to come with some word of Romeo—'Gallop apace, you fiery-footed steeds—' "

"Oh, Julia—" and Zoë de Rizzio tossed back her head and clasped her hands together. "Yes!

> Come, night; come, Romeo; come, thou day in night;
> For thou wilt lie upon the wings of night
> Whiter than new snow on a raven's back.
> Come, gentle night; come, loving, black-brow'd night;
> Give me my Romeo; and, when he shall die,
> Take him and cut him out in little stars,
> And he will make the face of heaven so fine
> That all the world will be in love with night
> And pay no worship to the garish sun—

Julia was overcome—her throat tightened so that she could hardly speak. "Oh, Mrs. de Rizzio—" and then had to stop. But in a moment, "How can I ever say it like that! Why, it's as if you were thirteen again and yearning with your whole soul for Romeo to come. Could I—would you have time to see me after school until Thursday so that I can work with you? How can you say those words as if—"

"As if I were thirteen instead of in my sixties? But age only changes you on the outside, Julia. It's only the body that changes while, inside, we're as young as ever, eager as ever to love and to be loved, eager for the loved one to come to us. That never changes. And of course I'll work with you. How I'd enjoy that—back to the old times!"

All at once Julia was filled with gaiety at the thought of having two enemies—two to get the better of, to show her mettle to. "Oh, look at the time— I must go!"

And when she and Mrs. de Rizzio got up, she put her arms around the little woman, lifted her off her feet, and gave her a whirl.

"Dearie, dearie—never did I think you'd be able to do that—" And when she was put down, "You must call me Zoë. No more Mrs. de Rizzio." They laughed together like a couple of children, but now Zoë laid a hand on Julia's arm.

"Did you really call Oren by his first name when he was here? *I* never have—"

"Oh, I wouldn't have dared! I'd never even have thought of it. I just said Oren to Miss Dormody to get her goat."

"You wicked one! That *was* wicked, Julia," said Zoë seriously. "You knew what she'd say—"

But now Julia laid a finger on Zoë's arm. "And you do have the key to Rhiannon's house, don't you?"

Zoë de Rizzio gazed at Julia. "Why, I'd never lie—I told Lydia Dormody the exact truth and stayed faithful to my word to Rhiannon. Frank and I *don't* have it." Then a mischievous look came into her blue eyes and they sparkled. "But we know where it's hidden."

CHAPTER

11

They wouldn't hear finally until the following week, possibly Monday.

But Fran had been marvelous. Julia had to admit it in her journal where she could admit anything at all, even if it gave her a stomachache to do it.

Fran got up there on the stage—the last one to try out, and you had to wonder if she'd somehow cleverly arranged this so as to be the last impression the judges had, wiping out all other Juliets—and did the very lines Julia had chosen when she and Zoë had gone over the whole play to find Juliet's most dramatic and demanding scene. This had to be the one, they decided, where she is left alone in her bedroom after her mother, Lady Capulet, and her nurse leave, and she takes the potion Friar Laurence has given her that will cause her to seem as if dead.

Of course Fran would hit on that scene! Julia had stumbled once, but not Fran—she sailed through the whole thing, forty-five lines, which Juliet begins by holding up the potion in its vial and wondering whether it will work at all to keep her from being forced to marry Paris, when already she is secretly married to Romeo. Thereafter she goes on talking to herself, how she will be alone in the freezing dark, laid in the tomb full of family vaults and, because she might wake before Romeo comes, go mad.

Will she be stifled, or strangled by the loathsome air, where all the bones of her ancestors lie buried and where bloody Tybalt, "yet but green in earth, lies fest'ring in his shroud"? As she becomes more and more hysterical, picturing herself playing with the bones, plucking Tybalt from his shroud and with some huge one, dashing out her "desperate brains," she ends by thinking she actually sees Tybalt's ghost, begs it to stay in its purpose of spitting Romeo on its rapier's point, and takes the potion.

"Romeo, I come! This do I drink to thee."

Oh, it was hard—hard—to get that gradual, subtle rise of emotion from a healthy, natural fear to the beginnings of horror, to excruciating terror, to the edge of insanity, to actually seeing Tybalt's ghost—and then the drop back to that quiet, deadly determined, "This do I drink to thee." Julia had practiced it all again and again with Zoë, who'd been everlastingly patient, determined that Julia should get the part. But Fran must have been rehearsing with someone, too, because she had done it better than Julia. So Julia decided, miserably, sitting back in the auditorium alone, watching, with a pain like a stone in her middle.

And what was the difference between the two performances? She couldn't say exactly, because she wasn't down there next to Mr. and Mrs. Winter and the other judges, watching, listening to Julia and then to Fran. But in Fran there was a kind of firm assurance. Julia must have seemed younger, more nearly Juliet's age, she could say that for herself, more like a thirteen year old who's been pushed into a hideous situation too soon, though Mr. Winter had said that children weren't allowed to stay children for long in the 1500's. Even Julia's stumbling at one point had seemed a part of her too youthfulness. While Fran, never stumbling, but doing it all like an adult, seemed far older than Juliet at thirteen. She seemed in her twenties, and Julia couldn't put a finger on precisely why. But what difference would this make to the judges? She was almost as good as John. No, that wasn't true. She hadn't his warmth, and there was no comparison in their voices. Even though you could hear distinctly every word she said, hers didn't have his richness. And then the *way* he pronounced his words, thought Julia, the sound of each one. She couldn't describe it. It was as if he appreciated each one, the meaning of each one, but for Fran they were simply there to be said, even though she said them extremely well and got across the rising intensity of the scene so that at the end where she saw Tybalt's ghost, Julia got a crinkle down her arms even though she fiercely resented getting it. It happened in spite of her. And in the "gallop apace" scene—well, Fran must have been thinking of whatever college man she was going with at present. She wanted him.

She and John would be doing the parts. And Julia? John came up to her afterwards from down in front where he'd been standing with a little group around Fran, who'd been making them laugh, and sat down and took her hand and said, leaning against her shoulder,

"Well, Miss Redfern, and will we be doing this together?" He had no doubt the part was his, just as he'd known he'd won the Greek Theatre Festival Award. He knew what he could do, what he was.

"No, you and Fran will. You know that perfectly well."

He flopped back. "No, I don't. I think Mr. and Mrs. Winter want you."

"How do you know?"

"I could tell from the way they watched you, and when you'd finished, Mr. Winter turned and looked at Mrs. Winter and raised his eyebrows."

"That's nothing. It only meant I'd failed and he was admitting it."

"Then I can only hope." But Julia had her head down and refused to turn to him, didn't dare look up she was so nearly on the edge of tears. He seemed to sense this because he reached over and took her hands again. "I have to go, Julia. Let's both hope," and he kissed her on the temple and got up and left.

He had a fearful long way to go—clear over to Alameda, where he lived with his three aunts who fussed over him, and they mustn't have had much money, you could tell, because of his clothes. Not as if that made any difference. John was John.

December 9

I'm being meanly jealous. Maybe it'll help to get all this written down, help to get rid of the irk and resentment. It reminds me of Mr. Winter saying those words of King Lear's about how sharper than a serpent's tooth is a child's ingratitude. Only I'm not talking about ingratitude.

Sharper than a serpent's tooth is jealousy. Fran is a queen bee, like Aunt Alex. They're a certain type, the kind of person who must be the center, who has to draw people around and get everyone laughing and listening to their stories. They want that kind of power, they must have it and can't rest until they do.

I've noticed how Aunt Alex gradually raises her voice at the dinner table when she has company or is at someone's house, until everyone is concentrating on her, and when she has them she keeps them. She's restless and dissatisfied until it's her voice everyone is listening to.

Fran's exactly like that. She doesn't always manage, but you can see her gathering her forces, having thought up some plan, bringing to school what she said were her "little nude pictures," and then having them passed around the lunch table and they turn out to be her baby pictures. And when she tells a joke and gets everyone laughing, she'll have one leg crossed over the other and at the final line, she'll twist the foot of the crossed-over leg so that she's pointing the toe of her shoe in. Always I see that toe going around and up the instant she gets a really good laugh, and she puts her head back and to one side and laughs along with the rest with her eyes closed, and brings her shoulders up as if she's thoroughly delighted with herself.

CHAPTER

12

"No, no! Not now, not now—your story first. Before we go on telling any more. I must hear the story—"

Rhiannon was on her bed, just as she'd been that other time, before Julia and Celia and Greg left the de Rizzios', when Rhiannon had come home from another journey and they'd had so much to tell each other. There she was, in her Japanese silk robe, curled against pillows on her huge bed, which stood at the end of this long room filled with eucalyptus colors, soft pinkish reds and grayed green, and the dark old family furniture, and sunlight. Julia had two pillows at the foot of the bed, and now she pulled her story from its envelope.

She began reading. And there were certain places, because this story was about Daddy, where her own words so moved her that she had to control herself, control the timbre of her voice, with firm determination out of sheer pride because she wanted nothing to interrupt the flow of the story and spoil it. When she would glance up occasionally at Rhiannon, she saw Rhiannon's eyes fixed on her face, never moving—but could not tell what she was thinking.

" '—and when his plane was struck, Harry felt it all through his body, and he exclaimed in silence, Julia, Julia, tell Mama I love her, and all of you, and that I wanted her to read my story and send it away. Then he saw the flames and climbed up out of the cockpit and leapt into the unknowing and uncaring dark, saw the javelins of fire knifing across the sky as if searching him out, saw the parts of his plane falling in blazing pieces around him. He fell endlessly through the night sky and his body was never found. And when they sent home his small belongings, the letters of his wife and children, Julia's letters all beginning 'Dear Father' instead of 'Dear Daddy' because he had gone away to become part of something so enormous that it was entirely beyond her understanding, those letters were not among them. Therefore it could only have been that he had them with him, inside his jacket, safe in his breast pocket.' "

Julia's hands, with the pages, dropped to her lap, and she looked up at Rhiannon. Rhiannon said nothing, only gazed at her, and Julia could not read her expression. Then, after several moments, in a low voice, "It would be 'tunic,' I think, Julia, instead of 'jacket'—yes, it would be—"

"But I thought a tunic was something loose, a kind of drapery—"

"It is, but in the war they called the soldiers' jackets tunics in the British Isles. I don't know why—"

"I see. Though Daddy was an American, so he'd think jacket. We're inside his thoughts." Julia waited. She felt sick. Her hands were icy, just as after her failure at the Greek Theatre, because no doubt she'd failed again. "You don't like it, then. Is it too—?"

"*Like* it! Where on earth did you get it? It's your father, of course, your own father. But how did you put yourself in his place, when he was killed when you were only six? What moved you to write this—what made you think to do it, write about his last moments?"

"I'm not sure. I had a dream about being lost in the hills, our own Berkeley hills, or so I thought they must be—one of the most terrible dreams I've ever had in my life. And when I woke up and was lying there in the dark, remembering the dream, I felt that my father was somewhere near—I felt this very strongly—and that if I went through the house I'd find him. Then gradually this story came to me, and I got up and began writing in my journal. Not the story itself, but my feelings."

Rhiannon nodded. "You've made me know that, how much the writing meant to you. I think it goes very deep and that you must have thought about your father's last moments many times. But how is the editor to publish anything this length? Isn't it too long for a young contributor, to go at the end of the magazine?"

"I didn't think of that, I just wrote. And if Mr. Clarke won't take it, I don't know what I'll do. Just keep it. Or maybe try to cut—"

"But you can't—not yet. Send it off! It's what it has to be. He'll take it. How can he refuse it! Oh, Julia, how exciting it is to be at the beginning as you are. I remember the way it was with Oren, and it makes me wish I could start all over again. But it's too late. Perhaps Lydia's right. Instead of shutting myself up with my music all my life, when actually I haven't accomplished much of anything, I should have been making friends. I've been too shut away—too shut away! And it's all my own fault."

"But you *have* friends!" exclaimed Julia, astonished. And then, after a pause, "Rhiannon, why does she hate me? Lydia, I mean? What have I ever done to her? I hardly know her."

Rhiannon studied Julia with a little curled smile on her lips, her eyes narrowed so that she looked, for just a fleeting moment, alarmingly, even though only glancingly, almost like Lydia—her face pale from her long journey from New York, with not enough sleep, her hair astray, and her eyes shadowed in their sockets. "She told me," said Rhiannon, "with enormous indignation how you called me by my first name, but not only that, called Oren by his, just as if you were an older, personal friend, and how impudent and cold and insulting you were. And how I should beware of you, worming your way into my confidences and good graces, a sly, nervy young one to be watched if anyone was." Suddenly Rhiannon's eyes widened and glowed and she leaned forward, extending an arm, and pointing an accusing finger at Julia. "Julia Redfern, what, precisely, are you up to? Ferreting your way into my home, getting letters from Oren Moore, the famous, the great Oren Moore, who has played before presidents and kings—*and* queens, I might add. Well, just one, as a matter of fact, the Queen of England. Shameless!"

Julia's heart had given a leap as Rhiannon leaned forward, arm outstretched. Her mouth had fallen open in shock; she couldn't believe—and then suddenly Rhiannon's arm dropped and her head went back. She hugged herself and rocked with laughter.

"Oh, Julia, Julia, you should see your face—"

"But that's awful," cried Julia indignantly. "How *could* you! And I didn't call him—well, yes, I did. Out of pure devilment because I wanted to get Lydia's—I mean, Miss Dormody's—goat because of all she'd said and the way she'd come right into Zoë's house without being asked when nobody answered the door. And Zoë said I'd been wicked. But you're not angry? After all, I didn't call Mr. Moore by his first name over here. You know I didn't."

"Of course, and it's what I told Lydia. I said I'd asked you to call me Rhiannon, and so she was put out, but then she often is, over something or other," and Rhiannon shrugged.

"But, Rhiannon, you still haven't told me. Why does she hate me?"

Rhiannon looked away and turned and turned the ring on her marriage finger, an opal, very large and full of fiery lights. She seemed to be trying to make a decision. "I think," she said finally, "that she feels you're too young to be such a close friend of mine. Too young, and yet old enough to understand things you shouldn't—according to her. She probably resents the way you come and go here, resents my feelings for you, which she has a very good idea of, resents the good times we have when it's very hard, practically impossible, for Lydia and me to have any good times together or any pleasure at all. She's too dissatisfied with me, and I've always resisted anyone who tries to direct me and constantly advises me. Oh, but, you *were* a wicked one to tease her about Oren!"

"His letter," said Julia. "Imagine! He said he'd been wanting to write me ever since he got back to Moorelands and that he wished I could come over to see it some time. He said he could still see me standing by the piano being Lady Macbeth and that he'd been thinking about ambition and my wanting to write. He said he knows about the disappointments and frustrations that come into your life when you want to do something seriously. Yet there's no point in expecting anything but the best of yourself. He said I'd be in his mind, and I thought that was awfully kind of him."

Rhiannon studied Julia for a moment or two, as if she were thinking over Oren's words. "I see," she said. Then, "I wonder how I can explain. I love my son dearly, but I know him, Julia, I *know* him. He's surrounded by people who flatter him. And though he recognizes quite cynically the superficial ones, the idle flatterers who only want favors, he feels rewarded by those who have a right to judge. He works very hard and will always have to, without letup. But because he needs to be admired, to be centered on, he put into his letter that he'd been wanting to write you ever since he got home, that he'd been thinking of you standing by the piano being Lady Macbeth, and will think of you—you'll be in his mind.

Julia! Don't take it all too much to heart. And then about seeing you at Moorelands and that perhaps you could come over some time. Really! At what age? And where would you get the money?"

"I know. I thought of that—"

"And what else did you think? What else couldn't you keep from thinking, given the words? You see, it's all—" but at this point Julia lost track of what Rhiannon was saying.

Fool! Because the thoughts, the imaginings had been there, just as Rhiannon, apparently, suspected they might be. And Julia's face went hot while she stared at her lap. The young girl arriving at Moorelands, the older man holding out his hands. "So you're here at last. How I've been looking forward to this, you can't imagine," and they would walk across the moors, talking, talking. He'd needed her to come (all very like *Jane Eyre*), and he would play for her at night, and then, after he'd played, they would wander up the broad staircase. Yes, but where is Rhiannon, where is she all this time while Julia and Oren are going for their long walks and he is playing for her and, late at night, leading her up the stairs to her bedroom where heaven knows what might happen? Somehow Rhiannon doesn't come into the picture, being inconvenient, not to say quite unnecessary.

"—but that's right," Rhiannon was saying. "That's sincerely meant, the part about work and the disappointments and frustrations that come of wanting to do something seriously, yet there being no point in expecting anything but the best of yourself.

"But, Julia, take the rest as it was meant, simply as a kind of apology for roughing up your hair just before he left when he was here, just after he leaned over and kissed you: another bit of thought-making, something for you to dwell on tenderly, or such was his impulse."

Julia looked up, hoping the last tinge of red was gone from her face. "Oh, well, of course—I know," she said lightly. "I knew perfectly well why he'd written the letter. It was nice of him, and I agree about the work. But I did know why he wrote."

"Good! Then I need not be concerned, yet he couldn't have imagined you'd be wise about it. And I won't have you misled."

Julia, feeling she must leave, got off the bed and picked up Rhiannon's medallion from the bedside stand. She held it, examining it closely, something she'd never done. It did not give up its beauty to the casual glance, but when you held it and looked into it through the surface carving, it was like looking into seawater. It was the color of seawater with sunlight playing in the depths and with strange shapes that came and went according to the way you turned the stone. The shapes were never the same, or so it seemed. What caused them? When you held it to the light and tried to look through it, it was more paradoxical than ever, turning to varying shades of gray-green, then pale, clear green, then golden green, and always it was haunted by its shifting lines and shadows.

"What kind of stone is it, Rhiannon? Something mossy. What do I mean?"

"No moss agate," said Rhiannon, "has ever acted like

that, and then, if a moss agate, it would be a kind of chalcedony, but no one I've ever asked has been able to put a name to my stone. I think it must be just some kind of random substance, perhaps fossil, that has been carefully cut and polished and carved, undoubtedly of no great value in itself. Only of value to me because Willie Yeats gave it to me and had our initials carved on the mounting on the back with the date of his giving it."

"Did your sister know him?"

"Oh, yes, knew him and cared for him as much as I did, I could tell, which was a bitter thing, because she hadn't even his friendship and his letters and his books that he sent me. He never seemed particularly aware of her, and he never wrote her, not once. But, look, my dear, it's getting dark and you must go."

She got off the bed and Julia put the medallion back on the bedside table, and the two of them went downstairs together.

CHAPTER

13

On this fresh, gray San Francisco morning, Julia swung off the streetcar at Park Praesidio and walked over toward the dark mass of the park and then along a block to the restaurant. It was precisely one thirty. The sun had begun to come out, and she felt suddenly full of assurance that all would be well. Exactly what would be well (she just might get Juliet, hovered the thought) she needn't stop to decide at present, and was filled with a pervading joy. Would Uncle Hugh read her story while they ate (but, no, she had too much to tell him about Lydia and about Rhiannon) or in the park? Probably in the park, or should she read it to him? She was perished, as she'd known she would be, and what would she have for lunch? Perhaps a toasted cheese sandwich with bacon, done crisp, and something rich and delectable for dessert. But she wouldn't tell him about losing Juliet and about how good Fran had been. No need to go into all that yet.

Uncle Hugh wasn't inside the restaurant waiting, so Julia asked for a table over by the front window where she could watch along the street for him.

When it got to be two and he hadn't come, the waitress began looking at her. Did Miss wish to order, the waitress finally asked, but Julia said no, gone hollow in her middle as she always did when she was sharply disappointed or worried. No, she said, but she must phone, and got her purse and envelope and went to the cashier's desk. Had a Mr. Hugh Tait called and left a message for Julia Redfern? No, said the cashier, a kind, worn woman who looked as if she'd be glad when the day would be over, but the dinner crowd was still to come. No, no messages for anybody. Was there a phone anywhere? This one, said the cashier.

Julia went behind the desk and tried to phone Hulda at Uncle Hugh's but the phone rang and rang in vain through the empty rooms. Aunt Alex was likely having lunch and a nice long afternoon gossip at Schrafft's with one of her friends, and Hulda out shopping. Julia phoned the art school. Was Mr. Tait around by any chance? No, said the girl at the desk, Mr. Tait had left at noon as usual. She hadn't seen him since. Julia phoned home, and after six rings,

"Greg—"

"Oh, it's you. Nobody's home. I've just gotten in and finally settled myself down in my cave with an extremely pleasant collection of food and some hot coffee, which is now getting cold, and you have to go dragging me, groaning and gasping, up that infernal flight of stairs when you know perfectly well I'm frail and elderly and must suffer *no* untoward exertions. What can you possibly want at this hour of the afternoon when you're supposed to be engrossed with our respected uncle?"

"Oh, Greg—I don't know what's happened. He isn't here and keeps on not being here. What can have happened! He *never* forgets when we're supposed to meet—not once. He just never *has*. I'm terribly worried, and he hasn't left a message for me—"

"Where are you, may I ask?"

"Well, at the restaurant, of course," cried Julia angrily. "Not at the art school, he hasn't, or at his house with Hulda, or anywhere. And it isn't like him. He's thoughtful. He *knows* I'd keep getting more and more worried. And he wouldn't just desert me—I know something perfectly awful has happened—"

Now Greg changed from annoyed old Professor Cranley back to himself. "Look, Jule, just the face the fact that he's—"

"*What*, Greg—*what*? There's a truck going past. Face the fact that he's *what*?"

"I *said*, face the fact that he's simply forgotten. He never has before. This time he has, for some reason or other. That seems to be the truth of the matter. So at least, if you look at it this way, sensibly, without going into a tailspin, there's nothing to worry about. Why don't you just eat and maybe somewhere along in there he'll remember and arrive, all embarrassed and full of apologies."

"I can't—I couldn't possibly eat. I'd be sick." Because she knew he wasn't coming, not if she waited all afternoon, he wouldn't.

If Mr. Tait should phone or come in, Julia told the

99

cashier, would she please say that Miss Redfern had stayed waiting for almost three quarters of an hour and that now she would be at their usual place in the park? She went outside, stared up and down the street, then walked slowly across into the trees.

These familiar paths she'd been taking with Uncle Hugh ever since she'd turned fourteen and Celia had decided there was no reason why Julia shouldn't cross to San Francisco alone. That is, provided Uncle Hugh met her at the Ferry Building. They were paths that led to that perfect enclosed space she'd discovered when she was eleven. Celia and Uncle Hugh would be lying on the grass somewhere, propped on their elbows, murmuring on and on to each other. Greg would be in the museum looking at the mummies, and Julia would have been wandering around talking to herself, being the owner of these parklands, acting out stories never written down because they were too long and complicated, coming into her head only to go right out again.

She'd turned onto this secret path, a short, hidden one, never discovered before now. And there was her Private Place, a stretch of lawn surrounded by trees and bushes that bloomed in their seasons, with a statue of a nymph or goddess of gray stone gone faintly green all over and deep green in the hollows under chin and breasts and arms.

She always thereafter stole up and looked to determine if anyone else was inside; if they were, she left. If anyone came while she was there, she ran off and hid in the trees until they had gone. This was her private world—people rarely found it. And then, after a while, when she came over alone, it became her and Uncle Hugh's private world, their rendezvous, their Private Place, to which they always retired after lunch at Buscaglia's to continue discussing important and special problems (mostly Julia's) or go on to other things.

And there always were other things. Such as: If God had created everything and therefore had control, why had He allowed humans to *be* sinful and cruel in the first place if He was going to visit His wrath on them for it? It was His fault they were sinful. And how could decent people go on living and be happy when other people and animals—especially animals, who couldn't speak for themselves and tell you what they were feeling—went on starving and suffering all over the world? It meant you had to be callous to put up with it, and it wasn't right to be callous, yet she, Julia, was often quite happy. And how could you believe that no sparrow fell without the Lord caring, and caring about every single human being, when He sent floods and earthquakes and fires and famines to destroy them in agony?

Such matters occupied Julia deeply for a long period when she was fourteen, and Uncle Hugh had no really satisfactory answers. But the fact that he'd wrestled with these questions too gave her some small comfort, because he was a sensitive, humane man. She'd heard Celia call him that once, sensitive and humane, and Julia thought those words described him precisely.

Now she kept on, up this path and along that one, the hollow turning to a gnawing ache in her middle, where

101

she felt all anxieties most painfully, all unconscious certainties that she refused to bring into the light.

She came to the leafy path, and then to that narrow opening which was the entrance to the Private Place and looked in. And there were Uncle Hugh and Nikki sitting in the full sun on a bench. He was leaning toward her, one arm behind her along the back of the bench and his other hand on his crossed-over thigh. She was sitting slightly forward, her hands clasped around her knees; she was speaking, but the words were too low to be heard. Now she leaned back comfortably and fully at ease, as if accustomed, within the curve of Uncle Hugh's arm that drew close around her, and he picked up one of her hands and kissed it, then let it go to run a finger down her cheek and throat. She turned her face to his and he leaned to her, tilting up her chin so that he—

Julia gasped and walked quickly away—oh, Uncle Hugh!—then stopped for a moment, leaning against a tree with her head down to get her breath. She was shaking. Perhaps all this time she'd known what had happened.

CHAPTER

14

She leaned on the rail of the afterdeck going home, now looking up at the snowy gulls, gliding swiftly by on the slipstream, close, watching her with their yellow eyes for a crust flung out, now down at the gray-green water hushing and lolloping past far below. But she saw neither gulls nor water. She saw only Uncle Hugh tilting up Nikki's chin so that he could kiss her. She saw him kiss her, that kind of long, drowning, satisfying kiss during which everything else is lost and forgotten, all promises, all responsibilities, obligations, all swept away, and their arms were clasped tight around one another. Julia imagined that kiss as though one were drinking at an upwelling stream after hours and hours of thirst.

Fools, fools! she cried to herself, almost weeping. To take that risk in the park, when any of Aunt Alex's friends might wander by. Anyone, anyone knowing the Taits. But who, what couple or single person, friends of theirs, would be wandering in Golden Gate Park or, if so, would likely discover the Private Place? The idea was preposterous. Those people didn't walk in the park or anywhere else, for that matter.

But, no, it wasn't *that* that was the cause of her anger. It was Uncle Hugh. He had forgotten her. He had brought Nikki to their Private Place, of all others, his and Julia's. That was what hurt most furiously. She would phone him—or perhaps he would phone her, on remembering. Yes, better to let him come to her. "Julia, forgive me. What can I say—?" "Nothing," she would answer, lightly and coldly. "What is there to say? Especially about taking someone else to our Private Place." Then what a silence there would be at the other end of the line. And after a moment or so, in a low voice, "Now there *is* nothing I can say." "I know. I can well imagine. And please don't ever ask me to meet you, or to go to the Private Place again. Because it's not private anymore, is it? Perhaps you've taken all sorts of friends there. So it's just any place, just nothing, just another part of the park and I'll never go there. You and Nikki can have it. And now, if you'll excuse me, please," and she'd hang up. And she'd never phone him again, and when they met at her house or over at his, she'd have nothing to say to him, and he would look at her—and not dare to speak. But inside himself—oh, Uncle Hugh!

She couldn't imagine such a state of affairs. She couldn't hurt him like that. It was unthinkable. Yet he'd hurt *her*. But not purposely. No, just carelessly, having forgotten her utterly, wholly taken up with Nikki.

Yet even so, the fact remained that she loved him, still loved him in the midst of her anger and bitter disappointment and probably always would, no matter what happened. Maybe he hadn't meant to do what he'd done; they'd been going along, he and Nikki, and he'd thought of the path and wanted to show her where he and Julia came to talk, because Julia had delighted in it since she was a child. And then the sun came out, and it looked so peaceful, so secret and beautiful with branch and leaf shadows moving on the grass, that they'd gone over and sat on the bench and gradually, because of the privacy and of all they had to say, things only to be said to each other—

Would she ever tell Uncle Hugh what she had seen? No, not possibly. *Vie privée.* She would never tell anyone, not Mother, not Greg. This would be their secret, hers and Uncle Hugh's, and he would never know that it was.

Now the ferry—as it had before it left the slip—gave its shattering bellow and Julia jumped and shuddered as she always did, as if she'd been shot. Looking up, she saw the fog drifting in thick across the bay, blotting out everything but a small space of water around them, a space that moved forward with them, continually surrounding them.

And all at once an arm was thrust into the crook of her own, leaning on the deck rail, and a face was pressed close to hers. "What's the matter, Julia?" came the unmistakable voice, and she turned and stared directly into the greeny-brown eyes of John Naismith, and he grinned at

105

her and put his hand over hers. "Didn't mean to startle. Say, your paw's cold! Give me the other and I'll warm it, too. I've been watching you for about ten minutes, and you hadn't moved by so much as an inch until the horn blasted. Were you thinking? Are you all right?"

She was silent, running around in her mind like a mouse snuffling out what it should do. What could she safely admit? "I was supposed to meet someone," she said finally. She had a need to tell just that to the right person at this moment.

"And nobody came. Was it a boyfriend?"

"Not in San Francisco!"

"Well, I'm relieved. I thought I'd been displaced."

"I never knew you were placed."

"Was it your uncle?"

Silence. "How could you know?"

"He lives in San Francisco, so you've told me, and that you sometimes do meet him. And I get that you're fond of him, that he means something special."

"Yes," and Julia looked away. "Mizzled," she said in a muffled voice.

"Now, there's a word I don't know."

"Mis-led. Mizzled, if you're a little kid and don't know any better. Mizzled by someone."

"Oh, I see. And your uncle was going to read your story. You told me you had a new one." John looked down at the envelope clasped to her chest along with her purse: the familiar envelope of that special size. "So it wasn't too difficult. Disappointment. Uncle Hugh not there. Reads all your stuff. No decision reached. Julia brooding at deck rail."

106

"In some ways you're so like Greg I can't believe it." Julia drew strands of hair from across her face. A freshet of wind had started up.

"Good—I like him. Shall I read your story?"

Julia swallowed and was at once assailed with all its probable weaknesses, awkward or possibly childish sentences, perhaps even sentimentalities despite Rhiannon's approval. Nevertheless she handed it to him, and he settled himself and began. Julia, beside him on one of the benches that ran under the railing, was shaking from cold, or nervousness, or perhaps both, leaning against him as if he'd been Greg. Absentmindedly, he put an arm around her and held her as if to keep her from shaking, but it was no use.

"Julia, I can't concentrate. Get up and walk and I'll call you."

After a while he nodded, and she came back to him, feeling sick, as she had at Rhiannon's, until she would know. He looked up at her without smiling and with the strangest expression, almost stern, which she couldn't read. "I like it—very much."

The blessed balm that drifts through the body like a physical warmth! Ego satisfaction? "You honestly do."

"Of course. I wouldn't say so otherwise. It's the best you've done." She sat down again and he put the pages back into the envelope and handed it to her. "How did it happen?"

She told him and he listened intently, then looked off as if trying to put it all together, to understand. "And no explanation—I mean no connection that you can figure between the dream and the story?"

"No. But for all this to come pouring out, some of it as if already written—somewhere!"

He was silent for so long that she put her hand on his arm. "What is it, Johnnie? What are you thinking? May I ask?"

"Just—that it's odd you should have written a story like this about your father after so long a time, that you should have been able to, as if it all happened last year. I've lost my father, too."

She felt a moment of shock. "But what do you mean? Just recently?" It was the way he had put it—the death could have been yesterday.

"Three years ago."

"And your mother?"

"She died when I was four. My father was often away on tour, so that's why we lived with the aunts, why I still do. He was their brother."

Again they sat there without speaking, but finally, "You said he was often away on tour, so then he was an actor."

"Yes. I always looked forward to his coming home, hearing his adventures—he'd act them out for us, and he had marvelous stories, I'm sure making them better for us than they really were, about the other actors and about the audiences and the difficulties. Getting through all sorts of weather to be on time at theaters way out in the boondocks somewhere. And I liked watching him work up his role for every new play, listening to him get his lines, and I'd do his cues for him. I felt awfully important as a little kid, reading him his cues—"

"So then you've always wanted to act—"

"Oh, yes, ever since I can remember. And I'd strut around after he'd gone off again, being Lear or Othello or Hamlet or Macbeth in the big scenes. It's always been part of my life. And it wasn't only Shakespeare. There were all sorts of plays. His company did repertory, changing from play to play on one run, with the actors all taking different sorts of parts."

She watched his face. He was looking down at his hands, gripped together, and she knew that he had loved his father intensely. And that his death had been a disaster—for a boy of fourteen. How had he died—why? But she couldn't ask as long as he hadn't offered to tell her.

Now the ferry was moving into its moorings, between the groaning and creaking piles lining the slip, leaning this way and that, as if in agony. And the gulls flurried up with a great rush of wings, then, as the ferry passed in, settled again along the tops of the piles whitened with their droppings. And were these the same gulls, now adjusting their feathers and gazing moveless across the water, who had ridden the slipstream over? Did they drift back and forth all day long, every day, the same gulls for each ferry?

John took her hand and held it as they, with everyone else, crowded forward to push through the cabin and out onto the foredeck. And the little, tough, bowlegged man, just as he had done when she was a child, tossed the ship's rope over the capstan on the pier, and they let down the gangplank and everyone began shuffling over.

"I used to look down," she said, "into the water between the ferry and the pier and be frightened of falling in." She felt John's hand tighten around hers as if he understood, as if he, too, as a child, had been frightened, looking down. "The same gulls," she said, "the same tough little bowlegged man, and everyone still going back and forth over the gangplank."

But the usual was forever being laid over with the new. Uncle Hugh had taken Nikki to the Private Place.

Now it was time to separate, Julia to turn toward the red train for Berkeley, John to go to Alameda. She stood looking up at him, feeling that he wanted to be silent.

" 'A thousand times good night!' " She was saying Juliet's words.

He studied her for a moment, then gave her a gentle little ironical tap on the nose. " 'A thousand times the worse, to want thy light!' " and turned and walked away with that curious, short-stepped gait of his. Up the street, far off in the school corridors, she knew his walk instantly.

December 12

Greg was sitting on his bed and I was in his chair in front of the desk, and we looked at each other. (I thought that I'd be writing about Uncle Hugh, what I feel, but I can't now. No use trying, it's too close.) "You went over to the park, to your usual meeting place, and then just came home." "Yes." And after a second or two, "You won't tell anybody about Uncle Hugh not showing up, will you, Greg?" and he said no, he wouldn't, that it was none of his affair anyway. Why should he? He thought that Uncle Hugh would phone, but I said no, he wouldn't, because he'd forgotten utterly. He'd likely never say anything and neither would I. And Greg gave me what I call his profound look, which makes me suspect he probably understands. He knows about Nikki being at the art school now, and how much the school means to Uncle Hugh—and about the past. And so I think he intuits what has happened and why I'm no longer worried about Uncle Hugh not coming.

I have a feeling that Greg and I, even though I get mad at him sometimes for being so self-contained and so often right, must be like Mother and Uncle Hugh. There's that secret communication. I've seen it happen. Their eyes meet and something unspoken passes between them. I must ask her if that's the way it's been since they were children. I think they understand each other completely—good night, little brother, she always says when he and Aunt Alex leave here after a visit, or we leave there, and Aunt Alex gives them a look. Wry, or perhaps sardonic, you'd call it.

Now the cats came into the basement through their cat door, just big enough for one at a time, that swings open with a flap that lets them go out or come in. They wandered over into Greg's room with their little welcoming cries just the way Patchy-cat used to when we were in the brown bungalow, and I picked up Sandy, my heavy, firm Sandy, all red-golden and glossy, his fur smelling of eucalyptus because the two of them love to hunt in the bottom of the ravine that must be cat heaven, with all its rustlings and privacy and surprises and electrifying lures for the chase. Greg picked up Gretchy and buried his nose in her fur and said how glorious to be a cat with no final exams and nothing to do but hunt for mice in the leaves.

Round about midnight Julia was still awake and into the fourth chapter of *Sons and Lovers,* found in the library on Shattuck after she'd gotten off the red train that afternoon, as if perhaps if she read more about lovers she might be able to understand about Uncle Hugh: the going back and forth, from wife or husband to lover. The ability to put on an act, to lie if need be, and to keep it up.

CHAPTER

15

Obviously Uncle Hugh hadn't said a word about anything. On Christmas day Aunt Alex laughed and exclaimed
over her presents and was delighted with the handsome
leather train case Uncle Hugh had given her. (And what
for Nikki?)

The tree was enormous and splendidly decorated as
usual. Uncle Hugh always did the top branches on a lad-
der, and Aunt Alex and Hulda the lower ones, Aunt Alex
unfailingly reminding them to be careful with her treasures, ornaments she'd had since she was a child. Christmas was Aunt Alex's season. The house must be filled
with candlelight; thick green fir swags must loop across
every doorway and window and mantel, sending out an
intoxicating fragrance; fires must be blazing; and the
two weeks before Christmas filled with parties.

Hulda came in, according to custom, to take part in

the unwrapping. But she had to get back to her kitchen, she always said, and looked flustered the whole time as she did each Christmas, her cheeks and the tip of her nose red and her movements quick and nervous. She could never rest lightheartedly on the warm, cushiony joy of receiving. "Oh, poor Hulda," Celia said afterwards. "I'm everlastingly thinking, while she's trying to be sufficiently pleased and grateful, let her go, Alex, let her go!" But, no, Aunt Alex must show Hulda all the exquisite things people had given her and Hulda must exclaim, until at last she is allowed to escape back to the peace and quiet of her own kingdom, from which excruciatingly delectable waftings could be caught of The Bird, twenty-five pounds of him, slowly bronzing in the oven. Really, it was as if Alex, Celia said, were actually twelve or thirteen at Christmas, what with trimming the tree, opening her presents which everyone must see and admire, and then eating an enormous dinner. It was a kind of orgy.

Greg was wearing his gift from Leslie, which Aunt Alex spied at once and buttonholed him about. Julia had watched him last night lift the lid of the small box that contained a set of scarab cuff links in something that looked like gold—"Gold-plated, they've got to be!" he said. "But they're so grand," said Uncle Phil, "and so striking and unusual, where will you wear them?" "To his wedding, naturally," said Julia, and knew that he would. His and Leslie's, one of these years.

But it wasn't this gift that sent him downstairs to his cave. He opened the fat envelope that came with the box and that of course, Julia was sure, held the four poems (together with a long letter, it must be) that Leslie had written for him, "Quartet for a Certain Young Man," about Nefertiti on top of his desk, about his room, about being homesick, about Greg's special personality.

He read the pages in silence, then went back and read them again, slowly, head down, so that his expression was hidden. She wouldn't tell him, Julia thought, that Leslie had actually begun creating them, the idea of them, right there on the pages of one of her letters to Julia. He'd want the whole thing private.

"Are they poems, Greg?" Celia asked. "Could we read them?"

He'd nodded, but as if he hadn't really heard, then got up suddenly and headed out into the hall, and they heard him thump down the basement stairs. No one would ever read those poems, Julia knew, no one but himself. . . .

"What is it, Julia?" came Uncle Hugh's voice, low, as if he wanted their conversation kept between the two of them, and she looked up, startled. She was seated around on the side from his place at the head of the table at dinner, next to him. "Are you all right? You've been so quiet today, not like your usual self."

"Have I?" She hadn't been aware of it, but had thought Uncle Hugh himself very quiet, very unlike *his* usual self. She looked at him, into his eyes. "I didn't know—maybe I'm tired from having read so late last night, and then I've been memorizing my lines for the play—"

"What's this, Julia?" demanded Aunt Alex, having apparently caught the one word from her end of the table.

"What's all this about the play? I suppose you'll have the part of Juliet—that is, if your little Mr. Winter can trust you not to forget your lines. That could always be a danger, couldn't it, dear?"

"No, Aunt Alex, not necessarily. I'm the nurse. A person called Fran Brinkley got Juliet."

"Ah! And that young Naismith," said Aunt Alex, drawing in her chin and smiling a certain kind of smile that meant she knew what she knew, "will certainly be Romeo. I can well understand your referring to 'a person' getting the part of Juliet."

Julia felt herself warming up at the back of the neck.

"I only said 'a person' because you don't know her. She's quite good and should have it. And I'm going to enjoy playing the nurse. It's not a role to turn up my nose at—she offers a lot of opportunity, actually. As a matter of fact." Aunt Alex scattered her own conversations with "actually" and "of course, the fact is" and "as a matter of fact" to lend force to her opinions, and even with "in point of fact," which Julia liked but would have felt silly saying.

"Perhaps," said Aunt Alex, "something interesting *could* be made of the nurse, but of course *Juliet*—! However, we must each of us recognize our own abilities and make the best of what we can manage." And she went on to give reminiscences of herself as a teenaged actress in high school, her highly successful portrayal of Portia in *The Merchant of Venice*, the compliments she'd received, the thrill of doing Portia's "It falleth as the gentle rain from heaven upon the place beneath" speech (unfortunately, or perhaps fortunately, these were all the words she could remember, so therefore couldn't give them the whole thing), and sharing her views on acting generally.

Meanwhile, under Aunt Alex's monologue. . . .

"But, Julia," Mr. Winter was saying, "you will take the part of the nurse, won't you? You have the touch for her, her liveliness and physical energy and all the teasing and bawdy remarks. You'll make it seem completely spontaneous. You'll enjoy it, and it gives the audience a chance to laugh in the midst of tragedy. See what you can do with it. It's not a role to turn up your nose at. . . ."

"Julia, what is it? I've lost you again." It was Uncle Hugh, and Aunt Alex was still carrying on about herself, and they were still having Christmas dinner.

"I'm sorry, Uncle Hugh—"

"Your story, I said. I thought you told me you were writing a new one."

"Not only were but did, and sent it off. I put in the final touches the night before last, about British and German planes and mailed it on the way over here. It won't go out, not on Christmas, but I had to have the satisfaction."

"British and German planes! What on earth—? And I didn't even get to read it. Seems to me I usually had the chance of reading your stories before you sent them."

"But somehow there hasn't been a chance, has there?" She watched him, watched his expression, as he blinked at her, seeming to reflect on this.

"No, Julia," he said slowly, "no, there doesn't seem to have been," and apparently had no memory at all of the

117

fact that they were supposed to have had a date at Buscaglia's with their talk afterwards at the Private Place. "And what have you been reading night after night?"

"Women in Love."

"I see—going right through D. H. Lawrence, are you?" and his expression never changed by so much as a shade. He'd made no connection whatever.

CHAPTER

16

December 25

Hello Julia:

Happy belated Christmas. I've just cleared up after Christmas dinner and The Aunts could hardly stand it because they have a certain way of doing things and fussed around until I chased them off. Probably guilt—the feeling that I wanted to do this for them because I'm not generally a clearer-upper. My Christmas job didn't bring in much. But I've got more gardening to do next week and maybe I can go on with it afternoons after school starts.

Anyway, I've heard from The Aunts' cousin in New York who says sure, to come on and stay with him next summer. Oh, I didn't tell you, did I? I've been thinking I must go to New York because of Dad. He died there and I want to see the places he talked about and the theaters he acted in and of course try to get a job acting in summer stock if I can. I got the idea of maybe staying

119

with Cousin Trevor because Dad was at his place when he died. Cousin Trevor, not just Trevor, The Aunts always call him. He was quite a famous journalist in his time and they're very proud of him and respectful. He said he'd be happy to have me, that he could do with someone to play chess with and do I play? Dad did. The weirdly typed pages of his letter reek of cigarette smoke. I guess most newspaper men light one from another. Something to do when the words won't come. Cousin Trevor's typewriter must be the first one he ever had.

Julia, it would be just for the summer. If I go you won't forget about me, will you? Or take up with someone else? I plan to hitchhike. Got to think about all this.

Do you, by any chance, think of me?
Love,
J

December 30

Dear Julia—

I don't know what to make of "Last Moments," about the man Harry in his plane, his "old bus." It astonishes me. But I don't see how I can publish it. I can hardly believe you wrote it, it's so different from your previous stories in the advances you've made.

I like the tone of it, the understatement, the fact that you've put in only small details that give conviction, such as the two or three names of German and British planes, the fact that the pilots called their planes their "old buses," that though they made so many flights when nothing much happened, they were intensely frightened most of the time and then so frustrated when nothing happened that the churning inside began until they got ulcers, and that when the Germans reached high altitudes they fired random shots to keep the grease in their guns from congealing. Good! Just these touches—enough to give us a sense of firmness under our feet as we read.

What I particularly like are the figures of speech, such as "the unknowing, uncaring dark" and "the javelins of fire" and Julia's reason for addressing her father in her letters as "Dear Father" rather than "Dear Daddy" as she would have done ordinarily. And then through the tone of Harry's thoughts, I somehow get his whole philosophy about the war—his hatred of taking human life, of committing an unforgivable wrong, yet his conviction of having to take a stand against an arrogant power.

If you can't in the near future write another story with just this sense of full realization, don't be discouraged. It's quite likely that you won't be able to, just yet, considering your age. But you will in time, I'm sure, because of "Last Moments." The ability is there.

What troubles me is that it's too long for the back section with the young contributors. I've made a few suggestions, along with the usual editing, for small cuts here and there. But it would really have to be cut further if it's to go in the League section. I'm sending the story back so that you can consider further cuts, then return it to me and I'll see if anything at all can be worked out.

Faithfully,
William Fayal Clarke, Editor
St. Nicholas Magazine

Dear Mr. Clarke,

I'm sure you're right about your cuts, but when I try to cut any further I make a mess of the story because it seems to me that what I'm cutting is really necessary. The cutting ruins my thought. So perhaps it's better for it not to be published at all than to ruin it just to make it shorter. I don't really know what to do. I don't suppose any magazine for adults would take it. What do you think?

I'm sending back "Last Moments" with sentences here and there lightly crossed out, or shortened, but this doesn't help at all. It's still too long and I don't want those sentences left out.

Sincerely yours,

Julia Caroline Redfern

There was a knock at the door, it opened, and Celia put her head in. "Julia, what is it? I've called you to lunch twice. Didn't you hear me?"

Julia had her head in her hands and her elbows on her letter, which needed copying. But she hadn't the least desire to copy it. She had a feeling that nothing would be of any use.

"I've heard from Mr. Clarke and he says he can't take my story because it's too long—I've got to cut it."

"And have you?"

"No, it just wrecks it. I've shortened one or two sentences and even crossed out some, but it doesn't help. It's still too long."

"May I read it?"

Julia was sorely tempted; she longed to have Celia's opinion. All the same, "No, Mother. I want to hang on until there's no hope. I want to hear from Mr. Clarke once more."

"But maybe I could help. And you've let Rhiannon read it—why not me?"

Julia turned and looked at her. "Oh, Mother! Are you jealous?"

Celia gave her a quick, ashamed smile. "Yes, I guess I have been, knowing you've taken it to her twice. Why her and not me, I wondered, and was hurt after being given your others to read, first, before anyone. Even before Uncle Hugh. Why not me?"

"Well, it's just that I wanted to wait and give it to you and Greg in print—this one story, because it's different and means something special to the three of us. Greg hasn't read it, either."

"And Uncle Hugh?"

"But I haven't seen him, have I? He's been too busy. And then he's family and I'd like to save it for him, too, until it's in print—if it ever is. He seems to be quite occupied these days." Julia watched her mother's face, but Celia returned Julia's gaze without change of expression.

"You two haven't had a visit for some time."

"No, and I miss him. Did I ever tell you I've felt as if he's taken Daddy's place with me?"

"Has he, Julia? But I've guessed. How I wish Phil could sometime mean as much to you as that." Celia's voice was so full of feeling that Julia looked down in embarrassment. How could she say such a thing!

"I'm sorry, Mother, but he's too new." Yet it wasn't this. She couldn't imagine Uncle Phil ever, in any case, meaning to her nearly what Uncle Hugh did. It was unthinkable. "Uncle Hugh has meant something very special to me since I was a child. You know that. I looked forward so to every visit he made us when we lived in our brown shingle bungalow when I was little and when we'd go over to San Francisco. And he'd take me to the beach—remember? With a picnic that Hulda would fix? And then when we went to Yosemite, I could hardly bear it, it was so perfect. And there's the way he's always arranged every birthday lunch for each of us, you and Greg and me."

"Yes—Hugh has always been closest to me of all my brothers."

"Once," said Julia, "he told me something rather sad. He said that when we get something we've wanted for a long time, that so often there'll be a 'yes, but.' And when I thought about it afterwards, I understood. You and Daddy had each other, yes—but then he was killed in the war. Daddy finally got his story published, but he wasn't here to know it. I got my room with all the windows, but then I had to leave it after only a year. Uncle Phil finally got you, but there was Julia making scenes. I got to represent our school at the Shakespeare Festival with John, something I'd worked on for weeks, but I forgot my lines. And I've written a story Mr. Clarke likes better than anything else I've done and he wants to publish it, but it's too long for him to use."

Celia got up suddenly from the bed, where she'd been sitting, and came over to Julia and put a hand under her chin to lift it. "I hope that for you," she said, "there'll be a time that will be all happiness—a space of time. And Uncle Phil and I have each other and, as it turns out, you and he are getting along a little better together. Or so it seems to me."

"Yes. But please don't hope that he can ever mean to me what Uncle Hugh does. It isn't possible."

CHAPTER

17

They were at the Winters', the first rehearsal party. Already, in a previous scene, Mr. Winter had held up his hand, cutting off Fran in the middle of one of her lines.

"Frances, don't, I appeal to you, say to your mother, 'Madam, I am here. What is your will?' like a dignified old dowager. And don't say, later on, 'Come hither, nurse,' in that lofty tone and with that insulting, impatient, beckoning waggle of the first two fingers as if you were getting a lowly clerk into your office. Your nurse isn't some peasant, nameless *thing*. I think you love her far better than your mother, someone you have to call Madam."

Now they were talking about another scene, and Fran seemed to be having the same difficulty. "When you say to the nurse, about her gossipiness, 'And stint thou too, I pray thee, nurse—' *don't* shrug up your shoulders, put your head on one side, close your eyes, shoot up your eyebrows, and cross your hands with the fingers spread outwards as if you were some deadly bored lady of fashion of perhaps forty. You will say those words impatiently, yes, but with a touch of humor and an implied love and understanding of the character of your nurse. And you'll say them like a young girl if we have to go over them twenty times."

Fran looked at him for a moment before answering, as she always did when he had a criticism of her. "But the nurse," she said patiently, "*is* just a servant, Mr. Winter, and Juliet *is* the daughter of the lady of the house." As if he'd never read *Romeo and Juliet* in his life! One thing you had to say for Fran, she had a special quality of bland gall. But Mr. Winter never got angry.

"Quite so, my dear. But their relationship is as I've explained to you. And Juliet is a child, not a woman. I want you to keep that in mind and play the part as I've directed. Otherwise you put the whole play out of balance. You make Lord and Lady Capulet's remarks to you as a willful and disobedient girl ridiculous, and Romeo as a boy under twenty as much so. I hope you see that—you have considerable intelligence."

Fran apparently thought this over with respectful attention, then seemed unable to keep from shrugging and closing her eyes in resignation with her eyebrows up, and the whole cast burst out laughing. Fran, not to be made a fool of, immediately laughed with them, as if she'd done it—shrugged and closed her eyes—exactly on purpose. She sank down on the couch and lay back as if exhausted, crossed her legs, and smiled around at everyone like a pussycat. And there, Julia noticed, there went the point of her shoe up and in, as if already Fran were telling this story on herself at a party after she'd been a triumphant Juliet, playing her role exactly as she saw it.

Now that the rehearsal was over, they were having sandwiches and cake and coffee. It was one of Mrs. Winter's famous chocolate cakes, with a firm filling and icing a quarter of an inch thick. There was a short silence while they cut into it and began eating.

"Gad," said Julia out of the stillness, "there's nothing like art and food together, is there?"

Everyone laughed again out of total sympathy, and she looked at them and thought how things hadn't changed much after all. Fran hadn't ruined the evening. She was over there on the other couch enchanting Will Moody, their lively, fun-loving but vulnerable Mercutio, who was quite gone on her, and she was making the most of it without mercy.

Julia was with John on the couch near the fireplace, with a good blaze going, and Mr. Winter on a footstool nearby warning her that she was going to have to fill her lines in the nurse's gossip scene with more color and shifts of emphasis so as not to bore the audience as much as she was boring Lady Capulet and Juliet. It could all be extremely funny if it was done in just the right way, and this made it always a challenge, even to a professional.

Now Mrs. Winter called him and he got up and went over to her. John and Julia, having finished their cake, took their coffee out onto the big porch at the back, where the cold winter moon was pouring a dazzling fall of white light through the lattice overhead. They put their cups on the old weathered table and John lifted her hands.

"Practical and strong," he said. "I was surprised to notice that when I first began noticing things about you. And I noticed the color of your eyes—bright blue."

"Dunderhead!" said Julia. "You're probably color-blind and nobody's ever told you."

John chuckled. "Reddish-brown—like your hair, but more brown. Do you, by any chance, know the color of my eyes or the shape of my hands? Have you ever noticed? Bet you haven't—bet anything. Bet you a kiss."

"Your eyes are greeny-brown and your hands are thin, not thin and long and useless-looking, but lean, as if they could do things, hard things. Maybe it's your lawn-cutting and pruning for the aunts. Am I right? Let me see," and she caught up one of his hands and examined it, holding it between both of her own. "Yes, I'm exactly right, and I don't owe you a kiss."

But she put her arms around his neck, he drew her close, and she gave him the kind of kiss in answer to his that she'd never given anyone in her life, opened her eyes and looked at him very seriously, very intently; closed them again and gave him another, and was filled with sensations she'd never before experienced—like nothing she'd ever imagined, that caused a blissful pain to run through her entire body so intense that she couldn't get her breath. Then was frightened and drew back. But John kept his arms where they were.

"Julia?" he said, and his voice shook. He, too, then. But "he, too"—*what?* The blissful pain?

"No," she said, and why did she immediately lie? "But what do you mean?"

"I only wondered if you felt what I did. But I guess not. Probably not."

She looked down and turned and sat on the edge of the table. "You're sure? You're so experienced you can tell in an instant?"

"I hoped you did." He lifted up her face and stood there searching it, then took her hands again. "I hoped you wanted me the way I want you."

"Oh—" and, then, when she could speak, "But it doesn't matter. Because I'm not going to get ahead of myself, ahead of what I can manage, I mean. And—and it wouldn't work. I'd hate it—"

"Not with me, you wouldn't, when we're older. But you're right, being infernally sensible. In some ways, I've noticed, you're emotional and impulsive, but all the same you have these sensible hands. So there's nothing for us but to wait. I had an idea it would be this way."

Al Morelli, John's faithful friend since they'd begun high school, always took John home with him in his broken-down car on these rehearsal nights so that John wouldn't have to go all the way over to Alameda or maybe even miss the last streetcar, and he'd drop Julia off on the way down. So there they were, the three of them, squeezed into the front seat with Julia in the middle, when all at once they began skimming crazily down these winding streets at breakneck speed, as if the little old car were either drunk or mad.

"Al—for God's sake!" John reached across Julia to grab the wheel as they lurched, squealing and skidding, around a sharp turn.

Al made no reply, and Julia had an impression of the black trees on either side not so much whizzing by as changing shape as if they were fluid. A streetlamp shone dully down at the end of this long, steep slope where the road curved to the left with a stone embankment curving with it along the far side, and there was a mass of darkness, bushes and trees, directly ahead.

"Into it, Al—into the bank—scrape it—!" John was shouting, but the car plunged straight on.

"Al, what are you *doing*?" and Julia turned her head and buried it against his shoulder, felt John on her other side throw himself across her with his arms around her, and there was a tremendous cracking jolt against something solid, together with the slashing and crunching of branches—and then—stillness.

John sat up and got out of the car, and Julia saw that they were surrounded by branches, through which a faint light shone as if from below. Al was slumped forward with his arms around the wheel and his head on his arms. "Al!" she cried, stricken with the idea that he was dead or unconscious.

But now he, too, straightened and got out and followed John over to a break in the tangle of shrubbery. They seemed, in the faint, confused light, to be looking downward, and Julia went to them and peered through the

131

leaves. What she saw, perhaps thirty feet below, was a solid stretch of cement patio with garden furniture and a garden lamp burning on a standard.

"Oh, my God!" That was Al.

"You damned, stupid fool," said John in a low voice. "What got into you? She could have had her face cut to ribbons, or been killed—"

Al turned on him. "What d'you mean, *Julia* could have been cut up or killed? Why just her? We could *all* have been killed—" his voice filled with passionate indignation as if he'd had nothing to do with this crazy happening. "It was the brakes. They went out. *Any*body could have told that. The brakes went right out on me." Then he turned and looked over into the abyss again. "Oh, God!" he said fervently as if he were praying. "Oh, God!"

February 8

I've been looking at myself in the mirror because of tonight. I so nearly might not have had any face—or so nearly might not have been here at all. I can't forget John saying to Al that *I* might have been killed—not that *we* might have been. He thought of me, and probably said it without knowing what he was saying.

Al left the car—there was nothing to be done about it until tomorrow morning, so we walked down, and John and I must have taken too long to say good-night up on the porch because Al, waiting out on the sidewalk, finally got fed up and said he was going on home and John could do what he liked. So John went after him.

I want to write here that something tremendous has

132

happened. I've always wondered what it would be like when I came to this moment. And when I look in the mirror and realize that it has actually come at last, my face goes different. It's probably pure happiness. I don't know how long it will last, but tonight is something I have to mark here in my journal for when I'm an old woman. And so I think of Rhiannon saying that she went to look at herself after being with Mr. Yeats, and was in despair because once it had been said of her that she was beautiful, but no longer.

CHAPTER

18

When Rhiannon finished Mr. Clarke's second letter, just arrived in response to Julia's, she looked up in amazement. "But it's something I'd never have thought of, that because he can't see where to cut any further, he'll publish the story as it is—ahead of the League section, and he'll pay you—"

Because the pale, clear winter sunlight was on the back of the house, they were in her bedroom again, Rhiannon in her favorite chair by the window with Julia opposite. And the direct light, falling across her, cast merciless shadows down her cheeks and around her eyes, so that she looked her full seventy-three years though her face was filled with delight over Julia's letter.

"I can't believe it, either. But remember what he said in his first letter, that I may not be able to do anything like this for a long time, being young, but I'm not to get discouraged. Of course I will! In a few months I'll be too old to send anything to him, then what will I do? I can't write the sort of thing they have in the women's magazines—"

"Then you'll have to keep on with what you *can* do, and wait. It won't hurt you. You don't have to publish at your age."

"Yes," said Julia stubbornly. "At least I think I do, now that I've—"

"—had this taste of success," finished Rhiannon. "I can imagine. Perhaps this Mr. Clarke has done you a disservice, but I don't know. Now you have something to measure yourself against." She looked away, but all at once, with complete unexpectedness, put a hand across her eyes. "Oh, Julia—I've never had any great, strong gift for being a concert pianist. I've seen myself all wrong, from the very beginning. And now it's too late. I've tried getting on with composing, but somehow the energy and persistence and perception aren't there. I had it three years ago—but not now." Her voice trembled. "Don't *ever* lose track of what you can do best!" And she got up and went to the window, and it was quite possible she was crying.

Julia, stunned, stayed where she was, though she wanted to go to Rhiannon and put her arms around her. But Rhiannon had turned her back, and it's cruel to make someone look at you in the midst of tears. And what was there to say to such sorrow, such regret?

"But how can you think you've failed," burst out Julia because the words had to come, "when you've had your music all these years and when you think what Oren's done and what he will do? Do you remember when I was over here one day when I was twelve and you said it might turn out I wouldn't write after all? And that another kind of life was just as important, to live with all my senses, you said, and to have a family? And I was furious because I thought that you, of all people, had failed me, and I said that to be ordinary was just dis*gust*ing, and you laughed and laughed because it was such a ridiculous word to use. And you told me the happiness you'd had because of Oren, and were you ordinary? Was my mother, or Zoë? Remember?"

Rhiannon stood still for a moment, then turned and smiled, and Julia went to her and hugged her, a strong, comfortable hug. "What good you do me," Rhiannon said, "give me back my balance."

"Do you know," said Julia, "my grandmother had a sharp edge to her—she didn't really understand me. I got on her nerves, and I knew she loved Greg best. He could never do wrong. So I've felt for a long time as if you're my grandmother. Do you mind? We're friends, but something more. Ever so much more."

Rhiannon looked at her with a mixture of wonderment and surprise. "Do you really feel that! I'm very honored, Julia. I couldn't be more so—" and there came a ring at the front door, a long, persistent one, and then two shorts.

"Oh, no—oh, my lord, it's Lydia!" Now the rings were repeated, just as persistently, as if Lydia knew quite well someone was at home and was not about to be put off. So down went Rhiannon and after the front door closed and there was a murmur of conversation, here came Lydia, *scuff-scuff* up the stairs, firm footsteps across the hall, and Julia felt frozen the instant Lydia entered Rhiannon's bedroom and those black, inimical, gleaming eyes lighted on her. Then, as Rhiannon came in after her, "Oh, it's *you*," she said. "Once again, it's you. I might have known, when what I want is to talk about personal matters with my sister." She turned and put her purse on Rhiannon's desk, took off her coat, folded it deliberately, lining out, and laid it over the back of the desk chair. Then she came and stood in front of Rhiannon and studied her—and was apparently shocked at what she saw. "Why, Rhiannon! Didn't you sleep last night? Have you had another of your headaches? Why, you look positively exhausted! And this child chattering away, wearing you out when you should be resting." She gave Julia the slightest shove to one side without looking at her and sat down in the chair opposite Rhiannon, where Julia had been. "Now, my dear, we must talk, but I'll get you some lunch first, and when we've eaten, you can get into bed and I'll stay for only a bit, but I've really—"

However, Rhiannon held up her hands as if to protect herself. Julia went over to another chair and sat watching.

"Lydia, I did sleep last night and I do not have a headache. And there's no need, ever, to tell me how I look if you don't approve. I asked Julia here for lunch, which is downstairs waiting for her to put it together. And she hasn't simply been chattering away. We've been discussing her writing. Will you forgive us, because we have a good deal more to talk about, the kind of thing that I'm

137

afraid wouldn't interest you very much. Would it be possible for you to come tomorrow when I have a free day?"

Lydia drew back, sitting tense and straight with her hands twisted rigidly together in her lap. Then she turned to Julia, but her look was leveled at Julia's midriff rather than her face. "Be so kind, young lady, as to leave my sister and me together. I have something private to say to her."

Julia got up and went to the door and closed it behind her. In the music room she sat in shadow on the couch where she and Rhiannon had waited with the tea things while Oren finished practicing. Now the sun had gone and this side of the house was dark. All at once she heard Lydia's voice raised as if in reproachful complaint or accusation, sharp and penetrating, going on and on for a long time, then lowered, then silent. And after several minutes the door of Rhiannon's room opened and Julia, with a convulsive shudder, saw Lydia come out with her coat over her arm and go toward the stairs.

For an instant she hesitated, and Julia's stomach tightened as she felt Lydia's gaze fixed on her. Yet couldn't be certain because of the darkness in the hall, while Lydia stood there, still as a figure caught in a spell, as if she were determining, in some stoney, purposeful way, whether to come into the music room and have out into the open some unexplainable crisis in her own mind for which Julia was somehow responsible.

But, no. She moved, she disappeared, and presently the front door closed and Julia got up and went in to Rhiannon. She stared at Julia with a look almost gaunt, as if Lydia had drained the very life out of her. Then she put her head back against the chair and closed her eyes.

"What I'm to do, I don't know. It's as if," she said after a while, opening her eyes again and looking out at the branches of the trees moving in the wind under a gray sky, "it's as if I have to put up a continual fight to keep control of my own life, to keep my private affairs private. I can never let up—the threat of trespassing is always there. And I won't give in. She's seven years younger than I, but I won't." Then, as if determinedly gathering herself, she got out of her chair. "At any rate, we won't have our day spoiled! Everything's ready—are you hungry?"

"Starved!" exclaimed Julia. "Look—it's almost one—"

And all at once Rhiannon put her head back and laughed, a big, wholehearted laugh. "Frustration and resentment always make me hungry. But, first, a thought. I'd like you to have the key to this house so that, if ever I call you and I'm not feeling well, you can come right in. Lydia wants to be able to come and go here as she pleases—'Oh, Rhiannon,' she says, 'your own *sis*ter, and considering those headaches of yours'—but somehow, I can't give in. However, this key I'm giving you I see as a symbol of our relationship. Yes, I like that—a symbol." And she went to her desk, opened the long drawer in the center, and picked up a key and handed it to Julia. "Keep it safe, my dear. It'll comfort me to know that you have it."

CHAPTER

19

Uncle Hugh's theory proved again—"yes, *but—*"

For some weird, incredible reason John and Fran and Albert decided to cut afternoon classes and go up in the hills in Al's car, that must of course have had its brakes fixed. If only it had been Fran and Albert alone, because the next morning the three of them were called into the dean's office and told that they were dismissed from the play. It didn't matter so much about Al as far as the play was concerned. He was one of the townsmen in the first scene of the first act who talked about biting his thumb at people. But John—

When he and Julia met in the hall after the three had had their dismissal and he told her what had happened, she had no answer, experiencing at once, in the pit of the stomach, that dread, shaming jealousy, like a sickness, that she should have been left out. "Would you have come with us if I could have found you?"

"Did you try?"

"Well, not too hard," he admitted with a little chuckle. "We thought we didn't have very long—that is, until we got up there and then it turned into the whole afternoon."

Silence, while Julia could feel him studying her, but she kept her face down. Finally, "You might have known," she said, "that you couldn't get away with it and still be in the play." She looked up and met his eyes, and he was smiling that ironic smile of his.

"To tell the truth, we never even thought. But how clever of you, Julia, to be so wise now. Do you mean you wouldn't have gone in a second if I could have found you and asked you to come, on such a day?" What he meant was that it must have been the first day of spring, or so it had felt, with the softest breeze blowing in from the Pacific. The hills were blue, as if bathed in a translucent wash of blue, and you could see every tree, almost every bush up there, as if they had been miraculously magnified in the crystal air. Julia had felt rebellious, as if she'd wanted to give a sudden silly leap like a spring lamb when she went outside at noon and looked up at the hills.

They'd said to each other, John and Albert, come on, let's not eat here. Then—there was Fran, who heard them, and she said, no, let's not, let's buy something and go up in the hills and have a picnic.

"Julia, the two things have nothing to do with each other, us, and my going off with Fran and Al. We didn't *do* anything, just bought some stuff and ate and lazed around in the sun and talked. Why should this make such a—"

But here came Mr. Winter, his little lined face grim,

his hair all tousled from having been scraped around, and he said, not looking at John, but only at Julia, that she was to be Juliet. And George, "our good George," that big, well-muscled, well-meaning but sometimes clumsy fellow, who'd played football last year until he'd hurt his knee and who had yearned, strangely enough, to be Romeo since the beginning, "is to get his chance at last." Then away he went, still not giving so much as a glance at John, as though he hadn't been there.

If it weren't for Mr. Winter, Julia was thinking, she would refuse to go through with it. But she couldn't bear the memory of that look on his face as he'd come out of the dean's office with everything fallen apart. No John, and the bitter disappointment, not just in the fact that the play was ruined because of the loss of John, but in John himself.

He laid his hand on her arm, but she pulled away and followed Mr. Winter out the door.

On Friday afternoon they stopped by Edie's Ice Cream Parlor on the way home after a session with Mr. Winter, five of the cast—Julia, Will Moody, and Gracie Manning, the new nurse, and Lolly Mallison and Twyla Vaughan, the Ladies Capulet and Montague. And there were banana splits all around with two scoops of ice cream each and plenty of chocolate sauce and nuts and whipped cream as usual, and they'd talked about Fran, which would have satisfied her, but of course she'd have expected it.

She was busy having a nervous breakdown. Couldn't

possibly come to school. Mrs. Brinkley furious, went to the dean, complained hotly of overreaction to an innocent childhood caper that had harmed no one, and couldn't begin to understand this intolerant, academic point of view. Principal, dean, and Mr. Winter holding firm. Then somebody called up the *Gazette*, a reporter came to the Brinkleys' yesterday afternoon when Mrs. Brinkley happened to be out for an hour or so, and Twyla, who had dropped by to have a little fact-finding visit with Fran, was lucky enough to be able to let him in. There was Fran in bed in her best nightgown and negligee, no lipstick, but with eyeshadow so as to emphasize the wide, sick, exhausted gaze.

Result: Juliet Devastated, read a small headline on the third page of last night's *Gazette*, down on the right-hand side.

Frances Brinkley, daughter of Mr. and Mrs. Herbin Baird Brinkley, lies ill at home after being informed by Roland Hughes, dean of the city high school, that she will not be playing the lead part of Juliet in this year's Shakespearean play, "Romeo and Juliet." The decision came after Frances was reported missing from her classes Wednesday afternoon. She had gone off for a ride in the hills with her fellow actors, John Naismith, who was to have been Romeo Montague, and Albert Morelli, to have been one of the townsmen of Verona, where the play takes place.

Mrs. Herbin Brinkley, prominent in Berkeley social circles, on being questioned on the phone, stated that her daughter is completely devastated after working long and hard on her part. Mrs. Brinkley informed this reporter that she will be in communication with her attorney because of her daughter's condition.

Pritchard Eaton, the principal, William Winter, instructor of the high school drama class, and Roland Hughes, the dean, agree that if such an escapade is allowed to go unpunished, all standards of behavior will suffer.

Neither Herbin Brinkley, owner of the Brinkley Insurance Company, nor Marsden Banks, the family attorney, were available for comment. Mrs. Brinkley says that she has no idea when her daughter will be able to return to school.

Twyla chuckled. "Fran was reading *Vogue* and *Harper's Bazaar* when I got there yesterday afternoon, or at least she had been because I saw them on the floor beside her bed. She said not to tell anybody."

"So of course you haven't," said Gracie.

"Oh, forgot," said Twyla, "Fran's parents are having fits about the reporter, my mother told my father, and I'll bet anything it was Fran who phoned the paper."

When Julia got home, she put her key in the lock and stood frozen with astonishment in the hall. For that was Aunt Alex's voice, full of anger and indignation; then Celia's, low, intense, reaching, coming from the living room. Julia went into her bedroom and closed the door, but the two voices slipped underneath when emotions rose. Words and phrases here and there in the flow of talk surfaced like jagged stones rolled up and then buried again in the current of a swift-rushing river.

"—*don't* understand!" This was Celia. Then Aunt Alex, "How can you deny it? Whenever I say . . . conspiracy passes between you. . . . Little brother, you always say! . . . children so influenced, even Greg. And, of course, Julia! . . . adoration of Hugh—" Then Celia, "But I've never *once* tried—" Aunt Alex, "—friendship with that Nikki Haydn . . . rubbishy little thing, I said . . . meant it, with good reason—" Celia again, "—amazed . . . student, almost penniless . . . sitting for Ted Haydn . . . some of the other artists . . . what possible difference?" Aunt Alex, "What difference, indeed! If you—" Celia, "—*any*thing but rubbishy . . . very opposite . . . intelligent, curious-minded, or Hugh would never have wanted to marry her—" Aunt Alex, who had apparently moved nearer the hall, "—foolish, impressionable young man, now a foolish, impressionable middle-aged man . . . will *not* divorce . . . my life literally finished . . . will *not* go through that miserable humiliation!"

Now Aunt Alex's heels struck sharply on the bare floor beyond the rug, then were muffled as they came past Julia's room. She opened and closed the front door, and Julia went to the window and saw her cross to her car on the opposite side of the street. Aunt Alex, in a dove-gray suit, with her big black hat set at its usual stylish angle and pulling on her black kid gloves, stood at the door of her car for a moment as if overcome by nerves or fury, then got in and drove away with never a backward glance.

If Uncle Hugh left her, she'd said—or that's what she'd meant—her life would be literally finished. What did *that* mean? That she would—? Don't believe it. Large, purposeful Aunt Alex finishing herself off for Uncle Hugh? For *any*body? No more busy life, no more delectable food, no more new clothes, no more parties and theaters and trips to Europe, no more chocolates in bed at night with the latest murder mystery? And with all those friends and all that money? And not because Uncle Hugh had gone back to Nikki—nothing to do with any regrets about Uncle Hugh at all, but because of the public humiliation.

CHAPTER

20

In the Saturday morning mail a letter from John and six copies of the April *St. Nicholas,* one for Julia as usual, and in a package one for Rhiannon, one for Zoë and Frank, one for Uncle Hugh, one for Leslie, and one for John. She'd written Mr. Clarke asking for the extra five, saying that she would pay, but he wrote back that on this special occasion, he was happy to send the extra copies free.

She tore open John's letter.

March 25

Dear Julia, who's probably at this very minute wrapped in the powerful arms of George in that gloomy auditorium:

I feel all at odds and ends. Do you know what it's like? *Awful!* I'm writing this in the public library and there's an old guy sitting not far from me with his head on the table on his crossed arms making the strangest sounds, whistlings and grunts and loud sudden snorts that rudely startle the rest of the herd and so of course somebody's reported him. He's horribly dirty and would I ever come to that one of these days when I'm old and out of a job, an aged, disintegrated actor of bit parts? (You can see how gloomy I am, having been a complete idiot.) The librarian's just come and shaken him awake and told him he'll have to sleep somewhere else. A few minutes ago she had to go into the stacks and haul out some poor creep who was kneeling down and looking through the stacks up into the woman's legs on the other side. She marched him off ahead of her and he never looked up once. He wasn't badly dressed either.

I miss you. You *are* avoiding me, aren't you?
Y'r obd't and r'sp'f'l sv't,

J

Oh, forgot—wit' love. Need I say? Yes. Because I do—you. Do you want to rehearse Juliet's scenes with me? Maybe next Sunday? I have to work Saturday. Shall I come over?

Julia stared into space for a full minute, then read John's letter over again. After a little she ripped open the package of magazines, took up one of the smooth, firm, fresh copies of *St. Nicholas* and flipped over to the back, breathing in the delectable fragrance of new paper and fresh ink, to behold "Last Moments." She read quickly through to be certain that all was as she had written, then went to the basement stairs to call out to Greg. But he was gone. Sharp disappointment. However, it was only ten and if she started at once she could get to the art school to catch Uncle Hugh before he left. In fact, well before he left so that she could meet him when he came out of his class at noon and give him the magazine, then leave at once. She wouldn't want him to think she expected lunch, not if Nikki were there. Yes, she would go. But first—and she drew out a sheet of paper.

March 27

Dear John,

Yes, I do know all about feeling at odds and ends—pointless, and yes, it's awful. As it turned out, I wasn't wrapped in the powerful arms of George because we haven't gotten that far. We're still stuck with me on the balcony and George down below, or supposedly, because there's no balcony yet, and Mr. Winter is driving him as if he was a big, stubborn sheep dog who won't learn to herd the sheep—or can't. We're all worn out with him, he wants so much to be Romeo but how he's ever to manage, I can't think. "You're in *love*, man, you're in *love*—make us *feel* it!" Mr. Winter shouts, sitting over at one side on that stool of his all hunched up, and when he shouts up come his fists, side by side, and he shakes them. You know! Then with such passion, he gets up and does the lines himself. And poor George does the lines again but maybe he's never been in love because he might as well be speaking to a doorpost—me.

If George can't make it, then I have a hunch Will is to be Romeo, but Will doesn't want to be, though he's probably told you. He likes his Mercutio lines—they're lots more lively and clever and sometimes funnier than Romeo's, full of wonderful pieces of wit. And he hasn't all that much memorizing compared to George. And Tybalt—short, broad, wicked Jess—doesn't want to be Romeo either and would look awful as Romeo but he's perfect for Tybalt. And so time's passing and we all know that Mr. Winter can't bear the idea of changing Will over because he's so perfect as Mercutio.

Oh, John, you *were* a dunderhead! Ruined everything, and I don't care a twit about being Juliet now. Not a tinker's curse. Yes, of course come over next Sunday. But can't you help George? You've got to. Somebody must, and you owe it to Mr. Winter. You could stay for dinner—not at George's, at our house.

Julia

At twenty of twelve, she was in San Francisco, climbing the rough wooden steps up the hillside in back of the art school. And as she climbed, blissfully reveled in one of her vivid imaginings, so vivid as almost to take the place of reality: of Uncle Hugh's face as he opened to "Last Moments"—*not* on the League page—and ran his eye down the columns of type. Then looked up, incredulous. He hadn't known anything of all this. It would be a complete surprise, the subject of the story, as well as what she had to tell him of discussions and decisions as to whether Mr. Clarke could publish at all, and if so, where to place it. "But, Julia, why is it here, on this page, and not in—?" There was so much stored up, waiting, while he'd been off, absorbed in his private affairs.

"Julia— *Julia!*" She turned and stared down the hill

to where Nikki Haydn was running up the steps. She stood waiting, uncertain and astonished. What could Nikki possibly want with her: Nikki, seeming so flurried and flushed in the face? "Julia, what luck to catch you before you disappeared and got beyond hearing. What luck you're here, to see you at all. Would you do something for me, something terribly important? I promised your Uncle Hugh that I'd meet him up there in the courtyard at the back of the school at noon, and now I can't. Would you give him this letter? You *will* wait for him? Had you arranged to meet him, too?" Anxious and tense she seemed, looking up at Julia from two or three steps below, and as if she weren't quite put together. Nothing Julia could have determined upon exactly, but so it seemed.

"No, he doesn't know I'm here—I only decided about ten this morning. My story's come in *St. Nicholas,* so I thought I'd leave it for him at the desk or maybe give it to him myself, whether we could have lunch together or not."

Nikki searched Julia's face. Then took Julia's hands and pressed the letter into them. "You *will* wait for him, be sure to see him? He must get my letter, Julia. You won't fail me." It wasn't a question, but a statement, almost a command.

"No, I won't. I promise you. Uncle Hugh will get your letter."

"Then, goodbye, Julia," and suddenly Nikki stepped up to Julia's level and put her hands on Julia's shoulders, kissed her on the cheek, then dropped her arms and turned and ran back down the hill to where, as Julia now saw, a taxi was waiting. She stood there, watching Nikki as she reached the bottom of the flight, turned to wave, then got into the taxi and was driven away.

Puzzled and depressed, Julia went slowly up the rest of the way, turned into the courtyard, walked over the uneven stones where weeds pressed up between, and sat down on the bench under the old peppertree, bursting out at this season of the year with clusters of tiny berries of glossy pinkish-red. "A very *shibui* color in Japan. Do you know that word, Julia?" Uncle Hugh had once asked her as they sat talking here and holding some of the berries in their hands. An understated and elegant color, he said. Subtle. She picked one of the clusters and held it, studying the berries' minute compactness and smoothness, their particular shade of soft red, and noticed that her hand was shaking and felt how she was cold all through.

Why should Nikki have promised Uncle Hugh to be here, then decided all at once to leave a letter for him instead? She must go inside, now, so as to be certain not to miss him. She put Nikki's letter into her purse—then felt a presence, and looked up, and it was Uncle Hugh. Without speaking he sat down and took one of her hands, then put his other over it. He looked tired and drawn, not at all as he had at Christmas.

"What is it, Julia? You didn't let me know. Why are you waiting out here?" And he glanced around as if searching for Nikki, because of course they must have had a luncheon engagement, and now, what to do about Julia?

"Uncle Hugh," and for some reason Julia's heart quickened as if she, like Nikki, were painfully anxious, "Uncle Hugh, I met Nikki on the stairs down there at the back, and she asked me to be sure to give you this."

His face changed in a breath from being vaguely concerned at her unexpected appearance to being plainly, almost sickeningly apprehensive: a wave of such devastating emotion that it brought that familiar tightness around his eyes, immediately, as he took Nikki's letter. "Excuse me, Julia," and he tore the envelope, roughly pulled out the pages inside, and read, his eyes obviously leaping from line to line, for within a second or two, by the crackle of paper, he was turning the page to read the next, then the next. Julia did not watch him (*vie privée*, if there was ever a moment to be called that), only sat there and, as he read, slipped her arm around his and leaned her head against his shoulder, looking down at the stones of the courtyard at a beetle making its way laboriously through the weeds.

When he had finished, he sat silent holding the thin pages almost crushed together in his hands. She tightened her told on his arm and brought up her other hand to slip under his arm as well. "Uncle Hugh—"

"She couldn't wait and face me—she was afraid I might dissuade her." It was as if he were making this clear to himself. "What did she say to you?"

"Only that she couldn't meet you, and that I *must* see that you got your letter and I knew how important it was. Yes, she said that exactly—'terribly important,' and that I wasn't to fail her. I promised her I wouldn't, and that was all. Then she ran back down the hill and got into a taxi.

153

Uncle Hugh, I'm so—I can't tell you," because she knew without explanation what had happened.

And when he got up and left her to go and stand at the back of the courtyard looking out over the bay, she sat where she was, so wholly concentrated on him in his grief that her mind was empty of everything else. She wasn't thinking, but was entirely taken up with feeling. She watched him while he shoved Nikki's letter into his pocket, then continued to stand there with his arms folded across his chest and his face turned away.

After a while he came to her and sat down, leaning forward with his elbows on his knees and his hands clasped in front him, so that still his face was hidden. "You said just now that you were terribly sorry, or at least it was what you meant. What do you know, Julia?"

She hesitated before she spoke, trying to decide what to say. But there was no point now in not telling the truth. "I know how it is, the whole thing."

"Did Celia tell you?"

"No, never anything. We've never mentioned it."

"But, then—?"

"You see, one day you and I had a date—before Christmas."

He seemed to turn this over in his mind, searching back, then groaned and put his face in his hands. "Oh, my lord, I remember. And so when I didn't turn up, what did you do, Julia? Go over to the Private Place?"

"Yes—"

"What must you think of me? Do you despise me?"

"Oh, Uncle Hugh, how could I ever? I want you to be

154

happy and I know you're not. I wish you could just go away, but something's happened and it can't be like that."

"No, I'm afraid it can't."

"What will you do?"

"Nothing. Continue as before. I have to earn a living— Julia, I wonder if you would understand that I can't talk. Not now. Shall I take you to the ferry?

"No, it's only a little way, and perhaps I'll do some shopping. I came over to bring you my story in print. Perhaps sometime you'll be able to read it and tell me what you think. Goodbye, Uncle Hugh—" and she put her arms around him and kissed him, pressed her cheek to his, and he took her hands and held them, then slipped the magazine under his arm and got up and started away. But turned for a moment.

"Remember, Julia," he said, "you're my girl, no matter what happens," and walked off toward the art school without looking back.

If he were an animal whose mate had died or been killed, she thought, he would raise his muzzle to heaven and howl with desolation. But being a respectable San Francisco banker, he could only go off alone somewhere and cry, quietly, so that no one would hear, then lie on his bed at home and think, his mind going around and around in the same tight and endless groove.

CHAPTER

21

Celia came into Julia's room just as Julia had been thinking about going out to help get dinner. She put down her book and Celia curled up at the foot of the bed. "I must have a word with you. That was Uncle Hugh who phoned."

"Yes," said Julia. "I thought so." She knew what was coming; she had a feeling of fatefulness.

"And I have an idea," said Celia, "that you heard Aunt Alex and me the other afternoon. You were here right after she left, but I couldn't talk about it then. I was too upset. Did you listen?" Julia nodded. "And why didn't you say anything?"

"Mother, I couldn't. Don't you understand? It would have gotten us into Uncle Hugh's affairs and then into certain things that are private—or were. Did he tell you? I expect he did, everything."

"Yes, of course. About forgetting to meet you at Buscaglia's and your going to the park afterwards and seeing him and Nikki in your Private Place, and then your going to the art school yesterday morning to give him the magazine, but having to give him Nikki's letter first. My poor Hugh. Yes, I understand your not saying anything."

"But he had to tell you, didn't he? I think you must have been always the closest to him of anyone except Nikki. Were you and he like that when you were children?"

"Oh, yes—the two youngest, separated from the other brothers by several years. We always stuck together and stood up for each other. I think there's always been something, some intuition, some feeling about each other that Hugh and I have always had."

"I know," said Julia. "It's the same with Greg and me. Mother, I want so much for Uncle Hugh to be happy—"

"So do I. I've wanted it for years, but how it's to be accomplished, I can't see. He brought it on himself."

"He started out all wrong, didn't he? Did you know he was making a mistake?"

"Oh, yes, I knew. But it was his decision."

"But, why, Mother, why—why would he have decided to marry Aunt Alex instead of Nikki? How could he!"

"Oh, Julia, wherever did you get that idea? It was Nikki decided against it. She was the one, because she was convinced they were of two different worlds entirely and could never be happy together in the end. And so Hugh, who'd been one of Alex's friends before he ever met Nikki, went back to her. A fatal mistake!" And she got up from the bed and came and put her arms around Julia and rested her chin on Julia's head. "I like it that you wouldn't say anything to me about Uncle Hugh in the park, nor about having to give him Nikki's letter. You left it to him. And you were quite right."

Julia, that evening, put the cats in her bedroom and shut the door so that there would be no interruptions, because they always wanted attention when you were on the phone or involved in some concentrated family discussion. They couldn't bear it, apparently feeling left out. Then, having told the story of her dream about the hills and about Mr. Clarke's arrival at his final decision as to just how to publish "Last Moments" in the main section of the magazine rather than in the League, she read it aloud to Celia and Greg and Uncle Phil.

After the last words, "Good, Julia!" said Greg. "Good for you. That's the best." And she looked at him and felt that firm, happy gratification she always did when she had his approval, which he didn't often express. She felt she could trust him absolutely, where Celia and Uncle Hugh might be swayed by their feeling for her.

Uncle Phil seemed to have no idea what to say outside of murmuring under Greg's comment, "Yes—oh, yes!" Perhaps, Julia thought afterwards, because this story of hers was so intensely about someone deeply loved in the family's past, someone whose place he had stepped into (you couldn't say "taken"), he felt an intruder at this moment into a private world, their private lives. Celia, too, was silent, her elbows on the arms of her chair, fingers clasped with her chin resting on them, her eyes closed as if she were still listening inside herself to Julia's reading voice. Then she looked up.

"Oh, Julia—it brings back so many things, it's almost too much." She seemed very moved. "And it's all a part of our other experience. Remember? When you were six, right after Daddy was shot down?"

"*How* is it?" But Julia half knew, intuiting that now, at last, whatever intimation she'd had right after her dream of being lost in the hills was about to be fully revealed and opened up.

"You mean," said Greg, "something to do with Julia telling you, when we got the news about Dad, that you must go through his papers and that he'd made Julia promise to ask you to? And you did go through them and found his story he'd been working on before he left— and sent it off and it was taken."

"But how on earth," exclaimed Uncle Phil, "could Julia at six tell you such a thing? What did she mean, her father had made her promise? When? Before he left?"

Celia shook her head. "No—he'd have told me, of course. And we never really understood Julia's saying that."

"It seemed to us then," said Greg, "as if somehow Julia had had contact with Dad, yet because all this happened after he went away, it could only have been a dream. Yet this still leaves the whole thing uncanny."

"Oh, but it *was*," said Julia. "That's what I've had in the back of my mind ever since this second dream made me write the story. You see, Uncle Phil, when I was six, I fell off a practice bar on the playground when no one was around, and a neighbor came and picked me up and kept me until I came to. And maybe it was then that I had that other dream of the hills. And it was Daddy who was with me, at least at first. And I remember we were walking together along a trail when he told me all at once that he had to go on by himself and that I must be sure to tell Mother to go through his papers, that I must promise him I would. Then it seems to me the trail turned, or at least I lost sight of him somehow. But why didn't I follow—why didn't I run after him? Oh, how I cried, because of the terrible loneliness, and when I looked around, I knew I was lost."

Celia stared at her. "So that's it. So it *was* a dream. But do we have what could really be called dreams in the midst of unconsciousness? Is that possible?"

"Maybe," said Greg, "Julia's was more what you might call a visitation."

Uncle Phil studied them in silence. He looked troubled, and Julia imagined how forcefully he was being faced with his own matter-of-factness in the presence of a certain subtle something that eluded him in these three who had become his own family.

"All of this," said Celia, "makes me wonder about what is really going on. Who knows, Julia, what's been keeping itself secret in you all this time? It's as if your childhood experience has been completed with this story."

"I know. As if I had a need."

CHAPTER

22

On Monday morning, "Julia, it's me—Rhiannon. I've been sick with the flu, and when Zoë wanted to come over I wouldn't let her because it wouldn't have been fair to Frank. So she got someone to come in, but the woman was a cold, meeching sort of person, all smiles and sweetness on top but cold as a witch underneath. Poor Zoë was appalled, but I'm much better now and don't need anyone, though Lydia's done some shopping for me and said why didn't I ask her to come instead of paying someone. Anyway, could you drop by this afternoon after school?"

"Oh, of course! I didn't have any idea—"

"I know, but I've been lying here thinking that I have to talk to you about something terribly important—"

"I'll be there, Rhiannon, as soon as I can. I have to stay for rehearsal for an hour or so, but I'll come right after."

"Good! Just get in with your key—don't bother to ring—and come right upstairs."

Julia gave John her letter when they met in the hall that morning before classes began, and he leaned over and asked in her ear, "Forgiven?" and she said, "For me, yes. For Mr. Winter, no," and they went their ways.

When they sat down with their trays in the cafeteria at noon, they began talking immediately and the food cooled.

"John, Mr. Winter doesn't look well. I'm worried about him. What's to happen to him, and what's to happen to us? There're only three weeks left."

"I know, and I've had an idea. It's the only thing I can do to help him if he'll let me— What would you think of my offering to handle the rehearsals for him if he'll stay home for a week, or the three weeks? I think he's getting something—"

"Probably the flu—Rhiannon's had it."

"So now, do you think the kids'll hate it, my rehearsing them? I know the play, and they know I do. They'd trust me, wouldn't they?"

"Of course they would. There're still a lot of rough places and we have to get the whole thing put together. What if you could get those rough places smoothed before he got back and then he could spend that last week rehearsing the whole play? Have you talked to him about it?"

"Not yet. So you don't think the kids would resent me?"

"No, I don't. It's just George—"

"I know—George. Isn't it funny! I have an idea he doesn't think much of me—not the athletic type, and all that—but if I hadn't done that damned fool thing, he wouldn't have the part of Romeo—"

"Which I think he's scared to death of now. He didn't know how hard it would be, all that memorizing, and being ordered around. He's terribly touchy."

"But I've got to do it—talk to Mr. Winter." John looked bleak. "I think it's going to be a rough three weeks. If it's the flu, Mr. Winter may not even be back in time."

That afternoon, Mr. Winter got onto his long-legged stool up on the stage and, leaning forward, knees bent with heels hooked onto the middle rung, hands clasped between his knees, searched their faces. Oh, yes, thought Julia, we were exactly right, John and I, to think he had to be persuaded to stay home. Under the hard glare of the work lights he looked exhausted, "gone," you might say, with great circles under his eyes and the lines down his cheeks more apparent than ever. He sat quietly until the chattering and laughter stopped—almost immediately, because, as they'd been asking one another, everyone in the play, "Why've we all been called together instead of just the ones for the scenes he wants rehearsed?" and "Why's John here?"

"My friends," he began in that not very loud and yet reaching voice he could use, "I won't waste time on preliminaries but just tell you at once that there's been another hitch." He paused, straightened, and put his head back for a second as if drawing breath, while groans and murmurs of apprehension ran through the cast. The old pro, thought Julia. He couldn't resist this little touch of dramatic suspense. "Oh, don't worry," he said, and chuckled, "the play *shall* go on. At least I hope so. But the thing is, I seem to be getting something, possibly the flu, and I have an idea I should stay home and get rid of it. A week has been suggested, and I think I must pay attention.

"Now, I'm trusting you'll cooperate with me so that I won't have to lie there worrying over the lot of you. Knowing you as I do, I'm reassured.

"To take my place, I've asked John to direct you. As you're well aware, he knows the play well. In fact, he has a thorough knowledge of most of Shakespeare's plays for the simple reason that acting runs in the family, and so I know I leave you in good hands. I want you to respect his word and if there's any difficulty or disagreement over some point he can call me and either Mrs. Winter or I can discuss the situation.

"Now, please remember the following, just in case I don't get back for our opening night, which will be three weeks from this past Saturday. First, all of you in the big roles, especially, but actually in any sort of role, go to the bathroom before you go onstage." Laughter. "Yes, I know it may seem humorous to you at the moment, but it's of appalling importance as any professional can tell you, and nervousness only increases the need when it finally hits you at the most unwelcome moment!" More laughter.

"Second, never stop watching people everywhere,

here at school, out in the city, in restaurants and stores, who might have anything at all to do, as to style and mannerisms, with the part you're playing.

"For instance, Gracie, in your role as nurse, watch little old dumpy women as they hurry along the street. Watch if they seem to fall onto each foot with every step—do they tilt forward slightly, or more as if their weight makes them sway a bit from side to side? Practice each way and see which feels right for you. Do they take little short steps, or the same as thinner people? How do they hold their arms when they talk? How do they tell a joke chatting with some acquaintance? How do they gossip? How do they laugh? Because your nurse laughs a good deal. Do their bosoms shake—and remember, we're going to give you a bosom. Watch their gestures. How do they sit down? As we do, carelessly, and without thinking, or do they have to plump down, often out of breath? And remember to practice still more intensively your gossip speech with Lady Capulet and Juliet to keep it as lively and varied as possible, this compulsive babble, on and on and *on*, to Juliet's exasperation but to the audience's delight. There's so much you can do with that speech! And of course the one where she keeps evading Juliet's desperate urgency to know where she's to meet Romeo and if he's even still alive. What opportunities for your imagination to take hold!

"Third, you Lords Montague and Capulet, be distinctly *different* old men. So far, you're too much alike. You, Montague, speak with a more lofty, stern, patrician grandeur. And you, Capulet, shorter, more open and direct, quick-spoken but easy and assured as if to show your position and power, give us all the same some sense of your temper, that thin skin lying there that makes you ready to turn with such sudden, brutal anger when Juliet defies you.

"George, I want to congratulate you on your improvement since the beginning. You've apparently been working on the marbles-in-the-mouth idea, which I recommended to all of you who were having difficulty speaking clearly. Practice it! Tiresome, yes, but remember how crazy with boredom you get when you can't, line after line, catch what some actor's saying.

"The rapier scenes with Mercutio and Romeo and Tybalt are coming along well, but they must still be worked on, all those movements like patterns meshed even more firmly. It takes a tremendous amount of concentration to get each one down to perfection so that you won't mess it all up on the final night and go through waste motions. It's got to be tense, and tight, and planned.

"Mercutio—but, no—John can handle it. Trust him. We've talked." All at once the last remaining impulse of energy seemed to have drained from Mr. Winter's body, and he stepped down from the stool, hesitated with his hand on it, then walked off across the stage holding himself upright with his arms out at his sides. You could see he was doing that: holding himself to get over to Mrs. Winter, who'd been waiting for him in the wings and now stepped out to take his arm.

"He's a sick man," murmured Twyla in Julia's ear.

John went down to the front row. "Everybody can go," he said, "except for Gracie and Julia and George. Mr.

Winter wants us to rehearse the first balcony scene. Julia, Mr. Winter would like to speak to you for a moment. He's waiting for you."

Julia, puzzled, ran up the stairs at the side of the stage and went into the wings. There they were, the two of them, Mr. Winter sitting and his wife standing with her arm across his shoulders. She'd been leaning down, saying something to him, but now looked up.

"Hello, dear," she said. "It's about George and what you can do."

"Julia," said Mr. Winter, "get a chair and sit down there in front of me, only not close." And when she settled, "Now, I want you to understand very clearly that unless you change your attitude toward George, he's going to fail. It's in your hands. You don't realize it, surely, but whenever you speak to him there's a kind of underlying flatness of tone in your voice, a coolness. You're fine in those scenes when you're with others, but not with George. This is a play of first love—my God, girl, make us know that! You say your lines to him with *acted* passion, but with no least love or tenderness. It's as if you're acting in some private little world of your own, looking past George's right ear and in love not with George at all but with the sound of your own voice, and even so, there's no real life in it.

"I know how bitterly disappointed you are that John was such a fool as to go up in the hills with Albert and Frances. I know quite well that this whole thing would be perfectly ideal in your view if only John had stayed behind and you could have been Juliet to his Romeo. But this is not how matters turned out. Therefore you must give George all the attention and fullness and depth of feeling you would have given John as Romeo. I know it's easy to say that. But unless you want to be a complete failure up there whenever you appear with George and unless you want *him* to fail, you're going to have to change. You completely inhibit him by your lack of emotion. Think about this. Stop being a little snob and looking down your nose at him. Go out there and give to George what you would have given John—the feeling. *Do* it."

Julia sat staring at him for what must have been a full ten seconds, while in the background she was vaguely aware of John being Tybalt to George's Romeo in the duel scene. Then she looked down, feeling sickish, her face hot with humiliation. He'd never spoken to her like this—calling her a little snob—as long as she'd known him. When she controlled herself, she gave him one brief glance, then got up and turned and walked off toward the stage.

"Julia." She stopped to listen to what he had to say. "You know it isn't just the play I care about, the play as a whole. If I didn't care about you and George, I'd never have said this to you. But I had to. I care about John, too, and he can't possibly direct you as things are."

She turned and looked at him. "I know that, Mr. Winter. I'll try. I promise you I will." She stood there a moment. "Go home and get well."

CHAPTER

23

She walked quickly along Grove toward Rhiannon's—already she had Rhiannon's key out of her purse. After she'd gone onstage again, she and George had done the first balcony scene for perhaps the fifth time. And she'd remembered with all her powers Mr. Winter's words and had spoken those lines,

> My bounty is as boundless as the sea,
> My love as deep; the more I give to thee,
> The more I have, for both are infinite—

with all the warmth and tenderness she could manage, putting everything into them she would have done for John, and apparently George felt this. He must have, because he responded as he hadn't until now, as he hadn't been able to.

And then John—oh, but what else could he have

169

said; how was he to know?—commended George and said he'd never spoken his lines better, then went on, disastrously, "But could I make two suggestions? First, try to pick up Julia on cue immediately she stops speaking, or even half a second before, the way we do when we're talking to people urgently. Unless we're thinking over what's been said and want to get our thoughts straight before speaking, we always answer at once, and when we're full of emotion, we're so eager to speak we can't wait. We interrupt—we overlap. And second, George, could you go along more quickly? It's the same thing, really. You're not slowly mulling over some intellectual problem. You're full of yourself and your feelings for Julia, and it all spills out. You have to be clear and you have to be heard up in the back row. But you're going to have to speak at about half again the speed you're going, otherwise it sounds too much like lines memorized instead of being forced out by the strength of your emotions. Let's go over it again so that you can give this idea a try."

But George didn't move. He stood there studying John, and then he said slowly, "I'll tell you what. Why don't you go to hell, you and your suggestions," and walked off the stage.

"—and what we're to do, I don't know," Julia was saying now, sitting on the edge of Rhiannon's bed, "because at last John knows—I mean, he *really* knows—that he doesn't stand a chance of being able to do one solitary thing with George. And he needs so much work yet. The minute Mr. Winter told us all that he'd decided to stay home and that John would be taking over as director, I looked over at George and he had his head down, and he never looked up once after that. I had a horrible feeling we were in for a deadlock."

"Your ridiculous, wicked John," said Rhiannon, "all his fault—"

"Yes, and now he's in a bog, a deep, thick, sticky bog. But what is it, Rhiannon? You said, 'something terribly important.' Tell me! Take my mind off the play!"

"Of course, and so that you can get out of here without seeing Lydia. She's been so good about trotting up and down ever since that other awful person I hired has left, and I appreciate it. But I so dislike being fussed and hovered over. I feel so terribly *watched*. How I want to be by myself, Julia! But, now, get me my jewel box, over there on the bureau. Not there? Then look in the top left-hand drawer. Good. Now pull up a chair right here beside me."

Julia put the jewel box into Rhiannon's hands and drew up the desk chair beside the bed. Rhiannon, smiling to herself, took out the old-fashioned clasped box she kept Willie Yeats's medallion in, and held up the medallion to catch the sunlight.

"Isn't it lovely—could anything be more so! And now, Julia, it is my desire to give this to you. No, no, don't look like that, all shocked and refusing. I've thought it over very clearly and left you the medallion in my will, but I want you to have it now, this minute. Here, lean over. Put your head down—yes, that's it. Now, go look at yourself in the mirror."

Julia went to the long mirror of Rhiannon's dressing

table and gazed at the medallion lying so strangely and unexpectedly on her perfectly ordinary cotton chest. Yes, but the dress she had on was the palest lavender, and the medallion did something surprising for that lavender cotton, lying against the rather high neckline: managed somehow, by its presence, to make Julia striking rather than merely fresh and attractive. Julia, feasting on its handsomeness, was keenly aware of what it did for her.

"Oh, but I can't take it, Rhiannon. I just cannot. It must be very valuable—"

"Well, no doubt. Not for the stone, so much, but because of Willie Yeats and his fame, and it will of course grow more so with the passing years."

"But surely it should belong to Oren. He'll expect you to leave it to him."

"Nonsense! We've never talked about it. And if I did leave it to him, what then? He'll fall madly in love with someone, give it to her on the spur of the moment, and then it'll be all over, their love affair, and she'll go off and take it with her. I'm running no risks. He might marry, but I somehow doubt it. He's so engrossed in his music I wonder if he'll ever take the time to think seriously about marriage. Affairs are easier, working as hard as he does. That way he has no lasting commitment, which takes time and attention and consideration and could result in children. No, Julia, I've decided. I've done what I want to do. I've had the most satisfying pleasure in our relationship, and this is my way of telling you what I feel. And now, come and sit down. I was turning over the pages of one of Willie Yeats's books last night and was about to start reading when I had to put out the light and go to sleep. Read to me a little, will you?"

And so Julia, the medallion swinging on its chain from her neck, took the book Rhiannon handed her and opened it, and it lay flat from long use.

"What shall I read?"

"Read 'When You Are Old,' one of the earliest ones. Read,

When you are old and grey and full of sleep,
And nodding by the fire, take down this book,
And slowly read, and dream of the soft look
Your eyes had once, and of their shadows deep;—

Julia took up the words, and their voices wove together, light and dark, soprano and alto.

"Rhiannon, do you remember the time I came over and you played for me for the very first time? You spoke of Mr. Yeats as if he were dead—I thought he was. But he's alive!"

Rhiannon laughed. "Oh, I'm like an actress. I get overcome with emotion. Willie wrote me something that hurt, some careless thing, reproving me. And so all at once, as far as I was concerned, he was finished, gone. For the moment, until I could forgive him. One of these days, I suppose, our letters will go into some big library's Yeats collection. For the present, they're in my strongbox at the bank. And now, read to me again."

So Julia read what she couldn't always understand, but the words sent shivers down her arms. Finally, she came to "An Irish Airman Foresees His Death," and as

173

always, when she read that one, her voice shook near the end so that she almost lost control, even though Daddy had not been Irish.

When she stopped, Rhiannon seemed asleep. She looked, thought Julia, very beautiful and rested. Quietly Julia got up, leaned over and kissed her, and her eyes wavered open, then closed again. "Goodbye, Julia dear. I feel wonderful, peaceful and pleased with my decision. Don't forget the little box it goes in."

"Goodbye, Rhiannon. I must get home. You know I thank you and that I'll be back."

She hesitated, apprehensive about keeping the medallion but wanting to do as Rhiannon wished. She got the box and went out and down the stairs. And she had just reached the hall when a key sounded in the door; it swung open, and there was Lydia Dormody with a bag of groceries weighing down one arm and the other curved around it.

She stood peering at Julia in the extreme dimness of the hall, for the sun was low behind the trees at the back of the house. Her abnormally white face was rigid with astonishment, her eyes enormous. Wisps of hair, escaping from under her hat brim, were all at sixes and sevens, and the collar of her coat was crooked because she had buttoned it amiss so that it was all hiked up on one side. She looked quite wild, as if she'd been forcing her way through a high wind.

"What are *you* doing here?" she demanded harshly. "How did *you* get in? Don't tell me you got my sister down here out of her sickbed!"

174

"No, I didn't. I have my key, the one Rhiannon gave me—"

"*Gave* you!" cried Lydia unbelievingly. "*Gave* you? What in the name of heaven for?" Now those eyes of hers in their dark caves fixed themselves incredulously on the medallion, which had been hidden by a fold in the blouse of Julia's dress. "Why, take that off at once!" she said in a low, penetrating voice. Then, more loudly, as if she couldn't endure the sight of it where it hung, "Take it *off*, I say! And what's that you have there?" She almost threw the bag of groceries onto the hall table and reached out, grabbing the little box and opening it as if she suspected Julia might have been making away with other pieces of jewelry. Then her fierce gaze went back to the medallion. "Give that to me—give it to me!"

"No—Rhiannon gave me the medallion. You have no right—"

"You are a wicked, wicked girl, to sneak into this house when you knew you were not to, with Rhiannon sick. Zoë de Rizzio phoned you, I'll wager, and arranged this. She's not to be trusted! I'll never trust her again, after I gave her strict instructions. Wicked and sly, that's what you are, and I've known since the beginning what you've been up to. Never think I haven't. Grandmother, indeed! What hypocrisy, and you took her in completely with your fawning and running in and out. But you'll never make me believe she gave you her medallion, her priceless, beautiful medallion. Never, never. You *took* it. You've always wanted it."

"I haven't— I didn't," gasped Julia. "I never did. I

175

never even thought of it. And she's asleep—we'll wake her."

Now there was a movement at the top of the stairs and Rhiannon was leaning over the banister, staring down at them. "What is it? Lydia, Lydia, what are you saying?" She had one hand across her eyes then, as if she'd awakened and stood up too suddenly and turned dizzy.

"Rhiannon, get back to bed at once," cried Lydia shrilly as if she were speaking to a disobedient child. "I *told* you to stay quiet and now look at you! You'll have a relapse after all my care, and this wicked girl has taken your medallion out of your jewel box, saying you gave it to her, of all the stupid lies."

"But I *did*, Lydia—I *did* give it to her. I want her to have it— She's telling the truth, and this is all too much, to hear you shouting down there, and now you'll be furious with me, and I'll have to listen to you, and it's all so exhausting. I can't bear it—"

At once Julia lifted the medallion on its chain from around her neck and put it on the table, looked up at Rhiannon and sent her a nod and a quick gesture of the hand, and left.

March 29

It was terrible—never anything so terrible as the look on that woman's face. I really thought she must be mad. I was so terrified of what might happen if I didn't take off that chain that I couldn't wait to get rid of it. What went on after I left, I don't dare think. I was sick at my stomach, so sick I don't remember what I said to Zoë when I

176

went over there. I don't even know if she went to Rhiannon's to try to reason with Lydia, but Zoë hesitated, I remember that—as if she wondered if she had any right. An outsider. Not any of her business. But of course Rhiannon had given Zoë a key, so that she could have opened the door, and Lydia will never forgive her, absolutely sure she arranged everything, that we're in league against her. But then everybody's in league against her—that's what she thinks.

I ran all the way along Shattuck to Vine, then as I climbed the hill, I kept going over and over that scene and thought of all the terrible things that have happened in my life after I could calm down a little. I don't remember going up the hill at all, and I was home before I knew it, lost in my thoughts.

First there was Uncle Hugh telling me Daddy had been shot down and would never come back. That was the most terrible thing of all, and Mother so sick we wondered if she would live. Then the fire, and me running down through the hills, terrified if I could possibly escape, and Dr. Jacklin's cats still shut up in his house, and poor Dr. Jacklin losing most of his paintings. And then, Mr. Kellerman, Addie's father, when they lived up the street from the de Rizzios', when I went over there and he heaved over the dinner table in a blind, drunken rage with all the dishes and food on it and smashed everything to bits. And after that, Daddy Chandler's death, and then me having to give Uncle Hugh Nikki's letter, and now Lydia accusing me of stealing from Rhiannon.

177

Mother and Uncle Phil and Greg are all out. The house is completely quiet. I wish they'd come. There's nothing to do until then—except, yes, phone Zoë.

Later

I've phoned and Zoë says she's phoned Rhiannon's lawyer—he was just about to leave—and told him about Lydia, how unbalanced she seems and that she must be gotten out of the house if Rhiannon is to get well. He's coming at once. And Oren's over here in this country on tour and will be in Los Angeles right after our play, which goes on April 17th. Then he'll be in San Francisco.

And so it could be I will see him.

CHAPTER

24

They'd had the house to themselves the entire Sunday afternoon, and Julia said she'd gotten more out of John's rehearsing her scenes with her in those four hours of hard, uninterrupted concentration than she had in all the time the cast had been working at school since rehearsals began. Of course Mr. Winter could give only so much time to each person, but now there'd been no one to watch and the two of them could put everything they felt for each other into those scenes.

"—but most of all it's because you were meant to be a director, John. You *will* be a director one of these days. Maybe rather than an actor, or both. But how can I go back to doing these scenes with George! Well, I must," and she made such a comical face that John burst out laughing and put his arms around her again. "I'll remember the sound of you saying his words."

At dinner that evening, Celia asked John how he'd managed to induce George to come back to rehearsals when George wasn't ready to take a single word of direction from him.

"Well, I knew I had to, and I knew George wouldn't listen to me if I tried to talk to him. So I did the only other thing I *could* do. I wrote to him and typed the envelope with no return name or address so that he wouldn't know who had sent it until he opened it, and then I hoped like Billy-hell he wouldn't tear it up and throw it away without reading it. And he must have read it, maybe out of pure curiosity, because there he was at the next rehearsal, not looking at me, acting as if I weren't there, but I didn't care. He'd come!"

"But what did you say in your letter?" persisted Celia.

"I said that he could go ahead and do whatever he liked—it was up to him, and that I'd never say another word. All I hoped was that he'd show up for Mr. Winter's sake, but of course for his own, too, because he had to be there or everything would fall to pieces including his own part in relation to everyone else's, and was that what he really wanted? After all, I said, he was the center of the whole thing—"

"Ah, you clever one," said Celia.

"And this is what's fascinating," Julia went on. "We know that George, at least for now, hates John, but when he got up to do his first scene with me, he was doing everything John had suggested—he was speaking faster, and he picked me up on cue at once, every time, or even a little before I'd finished, so as to give the feeling of someone who could hardly wait to answer. And it was

exactly what John had asked him to do, so he'd been rehearsing with someone at home and whether he knew he
was taking John's advice or not doesn't matter. Something's happened."

"And it's weird as the dickens," said John, "to direct
Tybalt in the duel scene with Romeo, for instance—Jess
and George—and to be telling Jess how to improve the
action, when I can't speak a word to George. He never
looks at me, just at Jess. But he's listening and apparently
he's applying whatever I say to Jess to whatever he thinks
will work in his own part. But of course it doesn't always
work—and I can see exactly how he could improve the
scene, yet I can't say anything. Mr. Winter phoned the
other night in an awfully rusty voice to ask how everything's coming along, and I didn't say a word about
George. What's the use? Or at least I want to see if I
can work things out myself without worrying him."

Uncle Phil had been quiet, perhaps listening, but
studying John consideringly as if he had something else
on his mind. Now they were talking about John going
off to New York for three months, and when Julia murmured to herself, "Three whole months!" Greg said dis-
gustedly, "Huh!" and Julia knew he meant the nine
months he and Leslie had been separated, and she
caught his eye and winked at him. Neither had changed,
he nor Leslie: they still wrote back and forth constantly,
and now Leslie had had enough of France, she'd told
Julia in her last letter. She couldn't wait to get home.

"Your last name's Naismith, John—is that right?" Uncle Phil asked all at once.

"Yes—"

"John Craighton Naismith," added Julia. "Impressive, isn't it?"

"But it seems to me there was another John Craighton Naismith," went on Uncle Phil. "Yes, I know that was the name. I remember him in my twenties, when I was going to *Macbeth* and *Hamlet* and *Lear* and *Henry V.* He was tremendous, the most famous actor I'd ever seen. None of us who liked plays would ever have thought of missing him, no matter how little money we had. Better to be up in the gods—the top row of the gallery—than not be there at all. And he was always billed with all three names, like Sir Herbert Beerbohm Tree, the great English actor—"

"Oh, lord, yes," said John, and gave a dry little shrug and one eyebrow went up. "You can bet he considered himself another Beerbohm Tree and always insisted that his billing should be with all three names, but as time went on, no one would have thought of advertising him any other way. But of course he wouldn't have considered himself *another* Beerbohm Tree. He was greater. He was *The* Great Actor of his time." And it was the way John said it, ironically—sardonically, even—that made them all look at him for a moment or two in surprise. "Oh, well," he said. "You've probably guessed it—he was my grandfather."

"When did he die, John?" asked Uncle Phil.

"Oh, about three years ago. He'd been living at some actor's club or other in New York after he retired."

At some actor's club or other, repeated Julia to herself. So though John could certainly have known, he didn't want to know, wasn't interested to know, hadn't asked, and nobody had told him. About his own grandfather.

"Did he want to retire?" asked Celia.

John gave a strange little half-laugh. "Oh, no! But that's what he had to call it. The truth was he'd gotten so hard to handle he couldn't be directed. He wouldn't take direction, so no producer was willing to take a chance on him. That was during the last six or seven years of his life. But he had been famous, just as you said, so famous that when he used to come and visit us now and then, if he happened to be playing in Oakland—San Francisco would have been much too much out of the way to come over—we couldn't seem to find anything to say. What could we say! What would have been of any interest in our lives to tell a man like that? Though he did all the talking, so it didn't matter. But when I was young, before he got too big an idea of himself, it was fun. He and Dad would do scenes together for us and it was marvelous." John stopped, and there was a waiting silence. "But, then—"

He had put down his knife and fork, and with his elbows on the table, was resting his chin on his fists and staring out of the window as if he'd lost this time and place and were in another. And he never did finish that sentence, and so Celia, seeing how it was, went on to another subject entirely.

But he finished it later, at about eleven that night when he and Julia stood together, pressed close with their arms around each other, up at the top of Vine Lane on Euclid waiting for the streetcar to come.

183

"Shall I go on, Julia? Could you bear to hear—about my grandfather, I mean?"

"If you want to tell me, I want to hear. Did it get too private? To go on telling at the table?"

"Yes. What I'd been about to say was that as Dad began to become known and admired, getting better and better notices, Grandad began criticizing more and more brutally—"

"*Brutally!*"

"Oh, yes. Without mercy. And it was crushing for Dad, because of course Grandad was *the* authority. But Dad didn't want to put on any more scenes with him because he knew it would only be an excuse for Grandad to tear him down. And then Grandad would say, "Oh, come on, Charlie, let's do—this, that, or the other—and we'll see how you're coming along. Maybe I can give you a pointer or two,' just as if Dad was some poor little unsuccessful rank amateur who needed all the help he could get when actually he was building a reputation for himself.""

"The old bull having to gore the young bull," said Julia.

"Yes. The old bull. The old jealous, watchful bull, boiling away underneath because his own son was challenging him—at least so he saw it. No room in the theater for the two of them. And when Grandad would come to see us toward the end, before both he and Dad died, Dad wouldn't be there. It was no use, he couldn't face it if he wasn't away on tour, that big, penetrating voice, that enormous, crushing ego, booming through our house, telling one fascinating anecdote after another about his meetings with the other famous ones, that we didn't want to hear about, but he never felt it—our hatred—because of his thick skin, and all that time the obvious condescension that the great man was coming to visit his poor, obscure children, and so kind of him!

"And when the aunts read in someone's interview with my grandfather that he had criticized Dad in public, pulling him to pieces the way he'd played *Hamlet*, they were so furious they were sick. If Grandad hadn't seen the performance, which he wouldn't have, how could he have known except for the two of them doing it together at the house when Grandad was still possible to be with? And of course Dad saw the piece in the paper in New York where he was staying with Cousin Trevor, and that finished him. Grandad's criticism had been eating into his idea of himself, and his last two performances hadn't been his best. My grandfather finished Dad's life just as if he had shot him."

"But John, what did he die *of*?"

"Of despair, the aunts would say. That's what they did say. Poor Cousin Trevor—he and Dad had been the closest friends. And so now I have to go and talk to him. I want to see where Dad was buried. I want to get as close to him as I can. Do you understand that, Julia?"

"Of course. You're a brave person, do you know that?"

"How am I? Why?"

"To want to go into that world, the theater, in spite of all this. How can you?"

"Because I'm myself. Not my grandfather, not my fa-

185

ther. I have my father's voice, so I'm told; that I always wanted to hear and that really got to me somewhere inside when he would say his lines. And I know what I can do. I can't go into any other world. It's where I belong, and I don't have my grandfather around to put me down. He's dead. He won't be hanging over me, criticizing me and making me lose my self-confidence. I'm not afraid. I know I have an ego, too—what George hates in me, I guess—but not a mean, cruel, petty one like Grandad's. I've seen what that kind can do." Julia put her face against his and kissed him. "Do you love me?" he asked suddenly. "You've never said it. You know I love you. *I've* said it." She couldn't answer. "Why won't you? Are you afraid you don't?"

"Oh, no, it isn't that. Not that at all. But I *am* afraid, of being hurt, I think—of hurting you. I keep remembering what Mother said to me once about Greg and Leslie. I said something about their probably being meant for each other, and she laughed and said, 'Oh, Julia, they're just children! How can you possibly know?' And I keep thinking of that. *We're* just children, I suppose, at least if they are—"

"Well, we're not adults, but we're not children, either. Far from it. But what difference does it make? We're here, in this moment. And in this moment I love you, and you love me but you won't say it."

"Then I'll say it, because it's what I feel. I love you, John. I do. And I'll write you all summer, just the way Greg and Leslie have been writing all this time, for nine months and three still to go. Yes, I do love you—"

And so they stood together in silence, feeling their closeness and that they belonged to each other, and would go on belonging—as far as they knew—from that time on. Then the streetcar came rattling around the curve and they tore themselves apart. John leapt up the steps and the rattling continued on its way, and Julia turned and went down Vine Lane, overcome with the strangest mixture of sadness and happiness she had ever known in her life.

CHAPTER

25

Julia phoned Rhiannon to ask if Uncle Phil could pick her up along with the de Rizzios about seven thirty the night of the play after he'd delivered Julia at school to get into her first costume and be made up.

"Oh, Julia, I'm not at all sure. I don't feel I—"

"What do you *mean*, you're not at all sure? Whether you're coming or not? But how can I be at my best if you're not there to make me measure up?"

"My dear, you'll have your Uncle Hugh and your family, and Zoë de Rizzio, and I'm just not—"

"Oh," said Julia. "Well, Rhiannon—I'm so disappointed. But if you really think—"

"No, Julia, I don't *really* think! I didn't realize how terribly disappointed you'd be, but I might have known. Of course, please tell Uncle Phil that I'll be happy to be picked up and that I'll be ready."

Julia, just before the first scene, arrayed in her costume for the Capulet banquet, looked out between the curtains and saw Rhiannon. You'd never have imagined she'd been sick with the flu. She had a new deep magenta dress with a high neckline, and that color against her ivory skin and the medallion on its silvery-gold chain and her big silver earrings were so striking that people turned to glance at her. She should have been an actress with her husky voice and her looks and her presence; it was a pity she never had been.

Uncle Hugh had brought Hulda, and there she sat, staring straight ahead but now and then turning her head from side to side with quick, stiff little movements like a bird's. She'd been so worked up with suspense and nervousness, Uncle Hugh told Julia afterwards, as to whether Julia might forget her lines as she'd done at the Greek Theatre, that her cheeks and the tip of her nose were bright pink as they always were in times of emotional stress.

But Uncle Hugh, when he'd slipped backstage for a second to give her a hug and wish her well, had been calm and quietly reassuring. He seemed in no doubt at all. All the same, if anyone had asked her to come up with this group of lines or that, she thought she couldn't have done it and dared not test herself. "But it doesn't matter," said Mrs. Winter, who would prompt from the wings on the right and John from the left. "They'll come when they're needed. Once in the swing of the play, you'll be all right. You'll see."

Yes, thought Julia, turning away from the curtains, but

there's nothing more sickening than this hollow uncertainty before the performance, the sickness and the icy hands. And to fail again—!

But she did not fail.

What she did—the secret of her being able to get through—was to keep hearing Zoë's voice in those scenes they'd rehearsed, and John's in the scenes where the two lovers are together. She kept hearing their voices, the feeling in them. Above all, the feeling. The present, here and now on the stage, had her in its grasp, but those voices were behind the words she was saying and hearing, bearing her up. George kept responding to her lines without hesitation or fumbling, and moved around the stage as if he was actually enjoying his part at last, enjoying the brilliant stage lights, the make-believe, how fine he looked in his costume with its red cape, and his awareness of the audience out there and that he was doing well. He was proud of himself.

And when the time came to work herself up in the vial scene, about to drink the potion Friar Laurence had given her, she paced herself, with every nerve aware of precisely how she was moving gradually from those first, quiet, fearful wonderings as to whether the potion would actually work, and how she could endure being alone in the dark tomb of the Capulets, on to a rise in tension, the beginnings of uncontrollable hysteria as she contemplates waking in that freezing blackness before Romeo comes, on to excruciating terror, near insanity, where she cries out to bloody Tybalt, still green and festering in the earth, to that utterly unhinged moment when she actually sees Tybalt's ghost, pleads with it not to spit Romeo on its rapier's point, takes the potion, and falls back on her bed.

She had done it—without stumble or having to search for a single word. She lay there quite comfortably with her eyes closed, feasting on the involuntary burst of applause that broke out after her last line had been spoken—done it all exactly as she had planned to do it.

But then the preposterous, the ludicrous thing happened.

She was laid in the tomb—tall, thick candles in immense brass holders (brought by the Winters from their home) at her head and at her feet, and with her draperies laid gracefully across her and falling in sculptured folds down the side of the catafalque onto the stones. And Romeo enters, finds her as one dead, swallows down the poison he has bought illegally on hearing that Juliet has taken her own life rather than marry Paris, and falls at her side. She comes out of her sleep, finds him lying there, steps down and kneels beside him.

> O churl! Drunk all, and left no friendly drop
> To help me after? I will kiss thy lips.
> Haply some poison yet doth hang on them
> To make me die with a restorative—

and kisses him.

And George kissed her in return. A good, loud kiss.

Oh, how Fran, if she'd been there, would have relished that moment! Everybody roared down in front and surely halfway back. No, they probably didn't roar, only to Julia's

191

ears. Probably some only snickered, but there *was* laughter, a wave of it, good, rich laughter, as if they were at a comedy and this were some kind of turn that had been planned. But in the face of this laughter, at the most poignant and moving moment of the play, Julia was thankful to remember later that she at least had had the good sense to wait. She stayed hanging over that abominable George as though imprinting his beloved features on her mind forever. And when everyone was quiet at last and the Watch had come into the tomb,

> Yea, noise? Then I'll be brief. O happy dagger!
> This is thy sheath; there rust, and let me die—

and plunged it into herself, folded over, and fell on him, and felt like giving him a good pounding.

"Oh, God, Julia," he whispered. "I'm sorry—I'm sorry!"

He was *sorry*.

What teasing there was afterwards, merciless teasing, after they'd all taken their bows and John was brought onstage by Mr. Winter for his share of recognition as the director who had taken over in Mr. Winter's place for the last three weeks. Then the curtains went across for the last time, and she saw John grinning at her. They'd planned it, everybody said, George and Julia, a nice, quiet, intimate little kiss, to play a private joke on the audience, only George had misjudged the force of his own passion. Or George had planned to surprise Julia. No, George hadn't planned it, but had been overcome. And by the color of his face, Julia had an idea this was the truth.

Wait till Fran heard, and she would have, of course,

by the next morning, Sunday. No, sooner than that, what with Twyla busy. Then there'd be other delectable phone calls back and forth among Fran and her friends, with the hashing-over and deep, throaty chuckles from Fran, and the profound satisfaction. Julia had been made a fool of, and Fran always won, one way or another.

April 18
Half past midnight

But in spite of everything, the Winters were pleased with us! I was having a stomachache over what had happened and being teased. But Mr. Winter said not to worry. He congratulated us, looking more lined than ever and very pale, but his old, lively little self. Mrs. Winter said he'd been like a feisty squirrel trying to get out of its hole these past few days, insisting on going back to his classes, but she wouldn't let him. Don't you worry, he said, it was only a momentary diversion and they only heard it down in front. Then he went off to comfort George, plain for everybody to see so terribly disappointed in himself after having put on such a good performance up until that fatal point.

We had a party afterwards, backstage, with cakes the parents brought, and I began to feel beatific, laughing and joking *and* starved, having two pieces of cake, different kinds, and knowing it was all over and that I hadn't failed.

Strangely, I've learned something about writing from being in this play. It's silent acting. I didn't realize it consciously until now, though I think I knew it in the back of

my mind. As I'm writing, I'm hearing and seeing it all—
the story—and it's like a play, because there's the dia-
logue and you're listening inside your head to just how a
person would say something. You have to hear the tone
and the way of saying and the rhythm, just as you do onstage when you're rehearsing your lines. And you're *seeing* it all happen. If you can't, how could you know
what each character is doing every moment, in relation
to the others, just how they're sitting or standing or turning and moving off the stage of your scene.

It's all so fascinating and unexpected—the way the
play experience has fitted in with the writing.

April 18

Julia dear:

We managed to catch the last ferry back to San Francisco, Hulda and I, and now it's one in the morning, but
I'm not in the least ready for bed after the play and the
party last night.

If your mother has told you about Aunt Alex and me,
you'll understand why I haven't been able to write you
since you gave me your story over at the art school. Your
Aunt Alex has decided that New York suits her far better
than San Francisco and has bought a large apartment on
Fifth Avenue, overlooking the park. We'll be selling the
house here and she will be getting a divorce. I'll go over
to Paris to get Nikki and bring her back when the decree
is final, and she and I will be staying at my old hotel—
you remember it—until we can find a place we'd like to
buy. Our living, of course, will be on a very different
scale than your Aunt Alex was used to.

And now to your story. I think you've always known how much your father meant to me. He was as much my own brother, I always felt, as if we'd been born into the same family, and so his death hit me hard. When I read your story, I felt the tears behind my lids, and I don't cry easily. I think that your father's death made a wound you won't get over, and that you'll express this in your writing in one way or another all your life, perhaps in ways you yourself won't recognize.

You've told me I've taken his place, but I don't believe I could ever take his place and I've never supposed I could, though I've wanted to be as decent an uncle as possible, and I've loved you as if you were my own daughter.

Which brings me to the fact that I failed you as a decent uncle and someone who loves you as his own daughter when I took Nikki to the Private Place. *Your* Private Place, because it was yours first and you took me to it because of the way you've always felt about me. I know that you've already forgiven me, but I must speak of it and say how very painfully I regret having broken your confidence in me. I never thought! How often careless people have said those three words. Nikki and I were walking in the park, after I'd forgotten my promise to meet you at Buscaglia's because of the state of mind I was in. As we came near the Private Place, I wanted her to see it and, without another reflection, simply took her there. Because of its quietness and beauty and its being so hidden, we sat down and began talking—and you came and saw us. Well, what more can I say? Nothing. Thank you for forgiving.

We'll have lunch and talk one of these days soon. And I'll be there. Can you trust me? Do you? And will you ever be willing to go to the Private Place with me again?

Your most loving
Uncle Hugh

CHAPTER

26

Zoë de Rizzio phoned a week later to say that Rhiannon had been ill only a few hours before she was gone.

"I was with her, Julia—she wasn't alone. She was talking about Oren coming to San Francisco and about you and the play ten minutes or so before I realized what had happened. She fully expected to be at his concert. I'd phoned the doctor to be sure there wasn't something I should be doing, because she seemed very weak, and he came at once. But there was nothing anybody could do. She'd just peacefully come to the end. I've let Mr. Moore know, or at least left word at his hotel. Everything now will be up to him."

Julia said something to Zoë she never remembered afterwards, then handed the receiver to Celia, went into her bedroom, closed the door, and lay down on her bed, curled up as if defending herself against such blows that come entirely without warning.

Over and over she relived two scenes, trying to find some way out of what she had done, some sort of excuse. And it had all been because of her emotionalism, her impulsive way of speaking out under the stress of unfair accusation, and then her persistence in impressing on Rhiannon how terribly disappointed she was at the possibility of Rhiannon not being at the play. She let out a muffled cry and put her hands over her face—but there was no way out. Nothing but to live with what she had done and the knowledge that Rhiannon might still be alive if it hadn't been for her.

Dimly she was aware of Celia's voice going on and on, sorrowfully, out there in the hall, that at length she hung up and was coming to Julia's room. She knocked lightly on the door, then opened it a little.

"Julia?"

"Yes—"

"May I come in?"

"If you want."

And so Celia came and knelt beside the bed and put a cool hand on Julia's cheek. "Julia, I know what you're feeling. It's so hard to accept, but at least she was in her seventies and had done what she wanted with her life—"

"No, she hadn't," said Julia in a level, remote voice.

"What do you mean?"

"She told me. She said she'd been a fool to stick at trying to be a concert pianist for so many years when she should have been trying to be a composer long before she began."

"But I think we do what we really want to do at the time, if we're free to. And if we're not, some of us struggle to. I think Rhiannon went on playing because she loved it—you know she did. And we most of us get fed up with ourselves at one time or another and think we should perhaps have been doing something else. And at any rate, we know one thing, what pleasure Rhiannon had in her son."

"Yes," said Julia, still in the same remote voice.

"You haven't been crying," said Celia, her fingers smoothing Julia's cheek. "I'm not a weeper, either. Tears have never been an expression of the depth of my sorrow."

Silence. And then Julia heaved herself up on one elbow. "Mother!" she said. "Mother—!"

"Yes, dearest, what is it?"

But Julia sank back again, knowing that she could never tell Celia what she had done. "Nothing," she said.

"But it *is* something. You want to tell me. Wouldn't it help?"

"No. There's nothing, really. I suppose I'll—"

"If you ever want to talk to me, please do. And you will get over this, Julia. I managed to go on living after Daddy was gone."

"Yes."

They sat in a half circle in Mr. Denby's office, Mr. Denby of Scrivens, Denby, Mortus, and Scrivens. He was a small man with heavy black brows that flew up to points on either side of his forehead and with large ears that went up to points, so that, what with his habit of keeping his head forward and looking up at everyone over the tops of his glasses, he gave an extremely gnomelike impression. He had a low voice and seemed to choose each word with care, speaking with the utmost clarity and precision.

Oren sat to the right of him, silent, remote, looking down at the floor, his hands clasped in his lap. He'd greeted Julia and Greg, Uncle Phil and Celia, and the de Rizzios most courteously, but he seemed, thought Julia, to be elsewhere. He might never have met her; there was no special recognition. Lydia Dormody sat next to him, pulling her chair close to his so as to separate the two of them very definitely from the others, to whom she sent not a single glance. It was as if, as far as she was concerned, they weren't there. She spoke to Oren once or twice in a private voice, but he gave no reply and did not look at her. She then settled her eyes on Mr. Denby, who was going carefully over his papers. At length he looked up.

"This is a rather unusual proceeding," he said after he was certain he had everyone's undivided attention, "to call you here to my office. Ordinarily I would get in touch with each of those concerned and inform them of the terms of the will so far it touched them individually. But it was the desire of Miss Dormody, the deceased's sister, that I call all of you here and read the will aloud. I was given no reason," said Mr. Denby drily, "but as it is not contrary to law to do so, I will, therefore, read to you Mrs. Moore's last will and testament, as follows:

" 'I, Rhiannon Dormody Moore, being of sound mind, do bequeath to my son, Oren Fitzgerald Moore, my entire estate, with the following exceptions:

200

" 'The sum of $20,000 to my sister, Lydia Eileen Dormody, together with my jewelry, except for my husband's ring and watch and other pieces in the jewel box so marked, the opal engagement ring given me by my husband, my wedding ring, and my opal necklace, so marked. These pieces are to be kept by my son, Oren.

" 'To my dear friends, Zoë and Frank de Rizzio—' "

But at this point, there came a high, harsh laugh. *"There!"* cried Lydia Dormody. *"There—*I *told* you!" and she was leaning forward, hands gripped around her alligator purse, and flashing a hard stare of triumph across the room at Julia and Celia, seated together opposite her. "I *knew* it was meant for me, and I was speaking the truth when I said that that girl had taken what did not belong to her! *Now* you will believe me—it was *exactly* why I asked Mr. Denby to—"

But at all once little Mr. Denby smacked his hand down on his desk in a gesture of angry outrage, having turned to Lydia as if he couldn't believe what he was hearing.

"Miss Dormody, I beg of you! We are here, in all solemnity, to learn your sister's wishes. For your own sake, if not for others', do not make a mockery of this occasion. Now, if I can continue quietly, I will go on." He was silent for a moment while he and Lydia glared at each other. Then, head up in stiff, stubborn pride, she looked slowly around at everyone and slid back in her chair. She glanced at Oren, but he had turned his head away. Mr. Denby cleared his throat and seemed to settle himself as if he had feathers to ruffle into place, then took up Rhiannon's will again.

" 'To my dear friends, Zoë and Frank de Rizzio, the sum of $5,000 in gratitude for all their care and concern.

" 'To Julia Caroline Redfern, another dear friend, the large desk with its chair, both in my bedroom, the eight books of poetry given me by William Butler Yeats and inscribed by him to me, as well as the carved medallion set in silver-gold and hung on a silver-gold chain, given me by Mr. Yeats and inscribed on the back of the mounting by him to me.

" 'This is my last will and—' "

"Oh, but it can't be!" Lydia Dormody cast her purse aside and rose up, stumbling over Oren's feet, and got herself over to Mr. Denby's desk, where she leaned forward to put her face as near his as was possible across that vast, neat expanse. "You can't possibly accept that, Mr. Denby! *I* refuse to accept it! Because she couldn't have meant it, Mr. Denby, not if she'd been well and known what she was doing. She couldn't have! It was that child's influence, calling Rhiannon her grandmother—what a brazen hypocrisy! She played on Rhiannon, on her feelings. Rhiannon was weak and ill, but she'd always meant the medallion and the books for me. Always! There was never any question—it was taken for granted, to keep them in the family. And I would leave them to—"

"Miss Dormody, please go and sit down—"

"Now just let me say what I must," cried Lydia. "Be that courteous. As I was saying, I would leave them to Oren, my nephew. We always talked of them as family possessions. What could that medallion, except for the money it would bring—and it would bring a great deal—

mean to anybody but me? *Imagine* giving it to a stranger who never knew the one who gave it to my sister. But I knew his poetry by heart, yet never even got a book from him, so now Rhiannon had it in mind to make up to me for all those years of keeping this great man to herself. Oh, I tell you—there was a power in her!" cried Lydia fiercely, her voice rising and beginning to tremble. "So you have no right—no *right*—" but here her voice went out of control and she burst into tears and covered her face with her gloved hands. Sobbing, she got herself back to her chair and sat down.

"Mother," said Julia, "I don't want—"

"I know," said Celia. "Mr. Denby, if these things mean so much to Miss Dormody, Julia couldn't possibly—"

Celia's voice went on, and the thought came to Julia that it was the strangest twist of fate that she should feel she must give what would have been her dearest possessions to someone who loathed her as much as Lydia Dormody apparently did.

"The thing is," she said, interrupting Celia, "I don't want to remember today like this—" And she got up and went out of the office to wait in the reception room for the others to finish.

After ten or fifteen minutes they all came out except for Lydia, who could be heard still talking to Mr. Denby, on and on. Oren Moore beckoned to Julia to come into the conference room opposite, and Julia got up and went with him, and he closed the door and they sat down at one end of the long conference table. She felt very formal in this cold room that smelled unopened, of the collections of magazines in holders and of all those books that closely lined the walls. The room was dim and Oren turned on the green-shaded lamp that lighted their faces as if they were paintings.

"Julia," he said, "I know exactly what you felt. It's regrettable—no, it's a disgrace to have to remember such a scene as that in connection with my mother's death. But she would be terribly unhappy if, because of my aunt, you—"

"But that's not really it, Mr. Moore!" exclaimed Julia. "I mean it's not the whole thing," and all at once, to her horror, she felt the urge to cry bursting up from her own chest as it had from Lydia's. She forced it back and looked down at the table until she got control, then up at Oren. "It's that—when I was standing in the hall after your mother had given me the medallion and asked me to put it on and then fallen asleep, I went downstairs and there was Lydia—I mean, Miss Dormody. When she saw it, she was furious, beside herself that I was wearing it and going away with it. She ordered me to take it off and said that I had stolen it, that I'd always wanted it, that it was nothing but hypocrisy, my telling Rhiannon I felt as if she were my grandmother. But your mother understood, Mr. Moore, because my own grandmother and I never got along—she never took to me, and Rhiannon and I had known each other for so long, ever since I was twelve, and we always had so much to talk about. I couldn't bear it—me steal from Rhiannon! And so I refused to take it off and Miss Dormody shouted at me, and I don't remember what I said then, but our voices woke Rhiannon and she came staggering out into the hall and begged us to stop. I wished I could have vanished. She was dizzy from having gotten up suddenly and come out, and I at once took off the medallion and left. I was so ashamed not to have taken it off in the beginning, so that Lydia wouldn't have had any reason to shout.

"And then Rhiannon phoned me, just before the play, and said that she didn't think she should come. No, she didn't get that far because I stopped her and told her how disappointed I'd be—I knew what she was going to say. And of course it was because she didn't feel herself yet, and was trying to tell me she felt she couldn't risk it. But I wouldn't listen—I refused to listen! That's why I can't— that's really why I—"

"You know," said Oren, "you've got it all wrong, Julia. My mother told me about the scene with my aunt, and she never once mentioned hearing your voice. But she most certainly heard my Aunt Lydia's. It was hers that woke her, she said, and then there was another scene upstairs after you left, something my mother always found the most hopeless and depressing thing in the world. As for her trying to tell you that she didn't feel well enough to go, she did. She said she felt fine, when we were on the phone when I was in Los Angeles, but thought she looked so awful after being ill that she wondered if she had the courage to let you and your family see her. That was what she wanted to tell you—then decided, when you were so disappointed, that she might as well wear her new dress and be festive—go to the play and be included in the party afterwards."

"And everyone thought she was beautiful—"

"I can imagine. I always thought her a beautiful woman. And so you will accept the medallion?"

"Of course. I never didn't want to. And if I have one daughter, I'll leave it to her. But if I have no daughters or several, I'll leave it to a museum. You can depend, because by the time *I* die, you'll—"

"Yes," said Oren. "Be gone long since."

CHAPTER

27

The five of them, Julia and John and the aunts, stood on the train platform over in Oakland talking small nothings—last-minute nothings, the kind that have to be gotten through because there isn't time to go into anything serious before the train comes. But then, all at once, when they saw it, very small and far off in the distance, John made up his mind and took Julia by the hand.

"Excuse us, will you, please?" and he drew her over to one side of the station and, behind a mass of luggage piled on a carrier, they flung their arms around one another and kissed each other goodbye, then again, and again, desperately, as if this were the last moment of all, forever. Now the train drew in and they came out from behind the carrier and there was Aunt Bea crying, but when John put his arm across her shoulders and gave her a quick, firm hug and said, "Oh, come on, now, Aunt Bea—I'm not leaving for the wars," she gave a sharp sniff and wiped her eyes. Neither Aunt Dode nor Aunt Win, taller than plump little Aunt Bea, looked in the least like crying, but each gave him a good, sensible kiss on the cheek and a pat, and then he ran up the steps of the train with his smaller bag, of the two he'd brought, that held his underwear and shirts, because he'd be traveling for three nights and four days.

He got himself a seat by the window and gazed out at them. They gazed back at him.

"Oh, this is the most ridiculous part of the whole thing—this long-drawn-out leave-taking," exclaimed Aunt Win impatiently. "Of course we want to see him off, and yet what is there to do? We should walk away this instant."

"Oh, *no!*" cried Aunt Bea, shocked. "We *couldn't*—"

"Walk away and leave and the poor boy in peace," went on Aunt Win, "not having to be polite and look at us, making the lot of us feel uncomfortable and useless, because the whole thing's over anyway. Absurd, I've always thought. But it's what one does."

Now John wasn't looking at the aunts but only at Julia. She stood under his window until the train began to move and then went along beside it, sending up quick kisses on the ends of her fingers until it speeded up and she was left behind. Just like that other time, she thought, when Daddy had to go to camp to be in the war and Mother walked beside the train until his window left us, and then I ran shrieking, *"Goodbye, Daddy—goodbye— goodbye,"* and Greg ran past me as if I were standing still and I hated him for it.

The aunts took her to the station restaurant to have coffee and doughnuts—"They have delectable ones here," said Aunt Dode, the one who had brought two upside-down cakes to the party after the play and who did most of the cooking at home. "Have you ever tasted them, Julia?" It was still only nine in the morning, and they'd had no time for a real breakfast, they said, though they'd tried to stuff John with one.

"So now he's really gone," mourned Aunt Bea. "For three whole months—"

"Well, he's not a child, Bea," said Aunt Win, obviously exasperated.

"Oh, I know, but *New York*—that *city*! And having to job-hunt from morning to night—"

"Well, he's practically eighteen, for heaven's sake. Time he got away, I'd say." You could tell how she must always be tilting against Aunt Bea's sentimentality, which must irk her to the bone.

Now, interrupting each other, or rather Aunt Bea and Aunt Dode interrupting Aunt Win now and then, they told Julia about Cousin Trevor, what a successful man he'd been in his time in the newspaper world, the journalism prizes he'd won, the places he'd been—all over the world—and now he was engaged in writing the story of his reporting adventures in three wars. "Got wounded twice," said Aunt Win, "but that never stopped him, and now he has a fine apartment in New York, and it'll be a real treat for John to stay with him. So fortunate, because we could never afford to put him up in even a small room for three months."

"And he and Cousin Trevor can talk about John's father," said Aunt Bea, "which is what John wants more than anything, it was such a dreadful blow to him—"

"Oh, I know," said Julia.

"Then John told you all about it?"

"Oh, yes, and about his grandfather, and he said he wanted to go and see his father's grave."

"Oh, but I mean," said Aunt Bea, "all those *pills*. Poor Trevor found the bottle," she murmured, looking away as if she were back there three years ago inside that moment when Cousin Trevor's letter had come—informing them of the suicide, Julia suddenly understood. Aunt Bea had crumbs at the side of her mouth, she saw in that rude moment of shock, and Aunt Win and Aunt Dode were staring at Aunt Bea in appalled disbelief.

Now Aunt Bea, in the silence, seemed to recover herself and turned her gaze back to them, coming to in aghast surprise at what she'd said, what she'd given away. At once she looked down at her plate without another word, her lips bitten between her teeth as if she were a child who has done the unforgivable thing and is trying agonizingly not to cry.

But Aunt Dode and Aunt Win went on talking briskly about John's acting and his highly successful directing of the play. And when, not much later, they were about to separate, Julia told them that her mother thought they must have a coming-home party for Leslie and John. Leslie, Greg's friend, she explained, had been in France for almost a year on her father's sabbatical leave and would be coming back at the end of the summer just when John would. So they could all be together again, all of *us*, she said. The aunts were delighted and for the first time since she had made her unthinking blunder, Aunt Bea looked at Julia with an expression that begged, "You *did* already know, didn't you, Julia?"

Well, my darling!

It was rotten, wasn't it? Our trying to say goodbye, but I care about The Aunts and I couldn't have asked them not to come, they'd have been so hurt all except Aunt Win. I could have explained to her but not to Aunt Bea. We had no chance to talk, you and I, or we could just have been together and not said anything. Been by ourselves—that'll always be the best.

How I'm to lie to The Aunts about Cousin Trevor, I don't know. He's so happy to have me here and tells me things he could never tell anyone else—especially not The Aunts, the whole story of Dad's last days, which I won't go into now. I can see it's a terrific relief to him and a comfort. He keeps reaching over while we're sitting on the old broken-down couch and touching my arm to emphasize what he's saying.

The broken-down couch is what I sleep on. Did The Aunts tell you all the wars he's reported on and the prizes he's been given and the wounds he's had and how he's honored at the Newspaper Guild and that all the other reporters respect him? At least the old ones who remember him. And that he's writing a big thick important book on his war experiences?

211

Well, that's all true in a way, but I think the book of war experiences has been sitting by itself for a long, long time now. The sheets are yellow and curled. How he keeps himself together or how what is kept together keeps going, I can't figure. He lights one cigarette from another and lives on sardines in a red sauce that he gets in big cans, boiled coffee that stands on the stove all day, and burned bacon. He doesn't really notice how he lives, surrounded by dirty dishes out in his little kitchen and by all the old newspapers and magazines, stacks of them, and millions of books gathering dust, piled all around the walls, that he loves like his children, and he keeps reading his favorites over and over, the big novels he can lose himself in, and he likes having me here because he can read parts aloud and slap his knee and exclaim how marvelous it all is, and did I ever hear anything like it in my life. And no, I never did, and I slide over and shove up the windows a little but after a while they're back down again because Cousin Trevor doesn't like drafts, which is what he calls a bit of fresh air.

Well, it was a blow, coming in the door, when all the time I'd pictured something elegant from the way The Aunts talked, with maybe even a housekeeper and Cousin Trevor's study all paneled in rich, dark wood and a huge mahogany desk with a thick rug on the floor and heavy draperies at the window to shut out the racket of the city. But small and shabby and dusty and crowded is what it is.

We've been out to Dad's grave and I put flowers on it. It's all I can do for him and I hope that somehow he knows what I've done, but he probably doesn't. Anyway, I can go back home now without his haunting me, the thought of him. I'll just remember how it was when we were happy together and he would say his lines for The Aunts and me and I could read the other parts for him to answer to.

Cousin Trev has recommended me to a friend of his who knew my father and admired him, and he wants me to come and try out for some small parts in five plays he's putting on. It's summer stock, which means repertory, a different play each week with the actors doing all the jobs. No money—just food and a place to sleep *and a chance to learn!* I go to try out tomorrow. The fellow they had for these parts is sick, and they're very small parts, Julia! But at least I'll be in with the rest of them—travelling around from one summer resort to another. By the time you get this I'll know.

It's late—I'm writing you on the little table, about three-by-five, out here in the kitchenette after clearing up all those dishes and putting everything away. Teed-jus! But I wanted to do something for him and he leaned in the doorway and read to me. Now he's asleep and snoring like Billy-hell. And suddenly I wonder with my face getting hot if *I* snore! I wouldn't know. Oh, lord, Julia, I hope not. I wouldn't want you to have to put up with that. I kind of think you purr, very softly once in a while. I'll love that. *I love you!* Write to me! I miss you and think about you, and the day I don't get a letter will be a black and empty one. I can't wait to see you again.

Your John, until death do us part—

213

My dearest—I miss you!

I had breakfast with The Aunts, and just as you guessed, they told me all about Cousin Trevor, or the Cousin Trevor they've imagined, and they have such an idea of him and how he lives that you can't possibly tell them the truth. I don't know how you're to lie to them, but you could skip the parts they'd never dream of but say how comfortable his place is and how much he likes having you there and what a fine time you're having together. If you have to tell them he has no housekeeper, you can say it's because he likes being by himself with no one messing around and upsetting his papers.

And so you've tried out for your first parts. If you've been taken, then other things will happen—if you're a success. Or can you be a success in such small parts? Does it make any difference unless the friend of your father might want you back again next summer?

I've been hit hard about one thing happening and then another. I've been down at the de Rizzios' and heard the news. They're going to move. And Oren Moore has sold his mother's house and now a family's moving in who will tear down the old windmill I told you about, where I used to play when I was a child, and they'll cut down the trees front and back that Rhiannon and the de Rizzios and I always loved. They're gloomy, the new owners say, and make everything damp. And Zoë can't stand the thought because now Rhiannon's house will be stripped bare and she'll see Grove Street and the streetcars and hear all the noise and they're going to paint the house tan (dog-do

214

brown, I used to call it) "with a nice bright green trimming," they told her, very pleased. A tremendous improvement, they think it will be, and they're sure Zoë and Frank must have been thinking all this time what a hideous old house it was and been ashamed to live next to it, and now it's going to be positively handsome.

Zoë said she couldn't trust herself to answer at first, then asked them if in their opinion Frank should cut down all the de Rizzios' trees. And the new people said they'd appreciate it because trees only make everything dark and cut up an awful racket in the wind, with all those leaves coming down, and drip after a rain.

Oren Moore doesn't know anything about all this, because a real estate agent sold it. He'd never have sold the house to them, because of the trees—for Zoë's sake.

Do you wonder why I've told you all this and what it has to do with us? Just change—that's all. I hope you get those small parts, because I know how much it means to you. But you'll change if you get them, spending the summer with these new people, doing what you want to do most of all. You say you can't wait to see me again, but John, that's what you say now, when you've been in New York only a few days.

I've been thinking of the things that can happen so that if they do it won't be so hard.

1. You'll get the parts, and the whole experience of acting, day after day, that you've never had before, will be so good you won't be able to bear the idea of leaving.

215

2. If you stay, even if you don't get another job right away, the idea of "wasting your time" finishing school when you could be getting some sort of part in regular theater will be too much for you and you'll keep trying.

3. You'll meet someone during the summer as in love with the theater as you are, maybe an older woman who will take a great interest in you, in one way or another, and you two will speak the same language. The way you and your father did.

I had some books to take back to the Winters and I told them what I thought could happen to you and they laughed. They said I had an entirely false idea of the theater in New York if I thought you could find a part in Broadway theater after the summer's over. Not at the age of eighteen. Possibly you might stay, they said. But they doubted it. You've got too much to learn. I had lunch with them, and Mr. Winter leaned over and patted my hand. "Don't you worry, Julia," he said. "He'll be back!" And I was cheered. After all, they're professionals, or rather Mr. Winter has been, in New York. He says it's very, very tough.

How strange to be so torn—to want you to be a success, and yet to want you to come back.

As I do!

I send you my love—
Your J.

Julia sealed and addressed the envelope and put on a stamp, then took up the last page of John's letter and re-read the words, "And suddenly I wonder with my face getting hot if *I* snore! I wouldn't know. Oh, lord, Julia, I hope not. I wouldn't want you to have to put up with that. I kind of think you purr, very softly once in a while. I'll love that. *I love you!* Write to me! I miss you and think about you, and the day I don't get a letter will be a black and empty one. I can't wait to see you again. Your John, until death do us part—"

Why, he meant it! Surely he meant it. And she heard Mr. Winter laughing and saying, "Don't you worry, Julia. He'll be back!"

She snatched up her letter and went into the hall, and there was Celia. "Why, Julia, where are you going in this wind? Haven't you heard it? You'll be blown away—"

"Going to mail something."

"*Some*thing—as if I couldn't guess! But why now? At ten thirty at night, when it can't possibly be picked up un-til ten or eleven tomorrow morning—"

"Don't care—going now—"

"Well, put a sweater on, then."

"Oh, Mu-uther! Who wants a sweater—it's glorious! I love the wind—"

Out she went, banging the door, and stood looking off for a second, in the face of that wild force, at the vast sea of lights which was Berkeley and Richmond, then dark-ness, which was the bay, then lights again, San Francis-co far off on the other side, sparkling and shaking as if alive, and turned and ran up the hill, watching the dark shapes of the eucalyptus all swept and flung about against the night sky, heard the stupendous roaring, and leapt up the steps two at a time, unaccountably joyous and hopeful.